On The Pitch

Book 1 in The Majestic Lions series
Michael Mabel

Copyright © 2024 by Michael Mabel

All rights reserved.

On The Pitch (Book 1 in The Majestic Lions series)

By Michael Mabel

No part of this book may be replicated in any form or by any mechanical or electronical means, without written permission from the author, except for the use of brief quotations in a book review.

This is a work of fiction. Names, characters, places, businesses, events, locales, and incidents are either the product of the author's imagination or used in a fictional manner. Any resemblance to actual person's, living or deceased, or actual events is purely coincidence.

Cover designed by GetCovers.

Contents

Forward	V
1. Kyle	1
2. Mark	4
3. Kyle	8
4. Mark	14
5. Kyle	18
6. Kyle	25
7. Mark	31
8. Kyle	37
9. Mark	42
10. Kyle	44
11. Mark	51
12. Mark	56
13. Kyle	67
14. Mark	73
15. Kyle	77

16.	Mark	89
17.	Kyle	97
18.	Mark	111
19.	Mark	117
20.	Kyle	124
21.	Mark	140
22.	Kyle	145
23.	Mark	154
24.	Kyle	157
25.	Kyle	163
26.	Mark	174
27.	Mark	186
28.	Kyle	192
29.	Mark	200
30.	Mark	204
31.	Kyle	213
Epilogue - Kyle		216
NOTE FROM THE AUTHOR		219
My debut novella		220
Blurb for Two Hearts, One Business: An MM Office Romance Novella		221
Michael Mabel		223

Forward

The book you're about to read is my first novel sized book, but second book overall. After publishing my debut novella, ***"Two Hearts, One Business,"*** I wanted to write a novel, and this is the result.
As I wrote this book, I came up with more ideas for some of the side characters. These characters will be getting their own books down the line. So, this book that I have written sparked an idea for a whole series.

The Majestic Lions series.

The series is about a group of players from a football team in Liverpool, England. Each book will feature a different couple and explore how their relationships form and grow over time. Some of the players will find love with another player on the team. Others will find love somewhere else, where they least expect it.

So, sit back. Get comfy and enjoy this sports themed friends to lovers story.

Content warning. This book does contain scenes of sexual imagery. Thus, this book should only be read by adults aged 18+.

Chapter 1
Kyle

"Damn, that was a good workout, Mark. I really worked up a sweat," I say to my best friend since secondary school.

"Ha, yeah me too. My muscles are aching now, especially my chest."

He isn't kidding. His chest is stretching the orange fabric of his gym shirt with each breath he takes. His tall, lean, muscular build has always been impressive to see, but watching him in action at the gym is another sight to behold. Mark is a machine when he's working out at the gym. He makes bodybuilders look like part-timers.

"So, what's it like being an apprentice plumber, with your dad?" I ask him, as we leave the gym and make our way to the car park.

"It's good, but odd at the same time. Most apprentices don't normally train under family. But it is nice to spend more time with him. Though, I could do without the boring details of what him and my mum talk about, and what they had for dinner."

His blue eyes flicker towards my direction, just as we make a turn on the pavement around the building.

"That will be us someday, unfortunately."

"God, I hope not," he laughs. His breathing is more relaxed now, just as mine has settled down to.

"I suppose working with your dad, you can't really bust out your usual sense of humour, which normally involves sex."

"True. Besides, not all of my jokes involve sex," he retorts.

"Err, they do. If the opportunity arises, you will still make a sixty-nine joke, like we're still back in school."

"Ok, you got me there," he admits, followed with a light chuckle, that always seems to lift my spirits, no matter the mood I am in.

"Enough about me. What's the latest with your marketing apprenticeship?" He asks me, just as ne near are cars.

"It's going good as usual. My boss, Stephanie, is amazing. I enjoy working with her. Plus, she's like the only one in the office who indulges me in my obsession with pop music. So that's good. The work I do is good, but it can be boring sometimes."

"Well, it sounds like overall you're happy, which is good to hear. I don't think I could work in an office. I need to keep moving, hence why I'm learning to be a plumber."

"And here's me thinking you were learning to be a plumber, so that you can be seduced by the lonely housewives when on the job."

"Now Kyle, don't go putting wild ideas in my head." He playfully smiles back at me. His smile is always a joy to see.

We reach our own cars and pull the doors open after unlocking them.

"Are you going to make it for footy practice tomorrow with the lads?" he asks me, as he tosses his gym bag onto the back seat of his car. We've been playing for our local team, The Majestic Hearts, since we left school. It's a great team to be a part of.

"Urm, probably not. I want to catch up on some work," I answer.

"Fair enough," he says.

ON THE PITCH

I settle into my car and wind the window down, which he also does in his car.

"Well, tell your parents I said hi," he says to me.

"Will do, and you tell yours the same from me."

"As usual."

We both lightly laugh, as this has become a 'thing' with us, as we're always at each other's houses, spending time with each other's parents.

"See you, Mark."

"Yeah, see you too, Kyle."

And with that, we both drive off and head out of the gym car park.

Chapter 2
Mark

"Hey fellas. I see you're all starting without me," I say upon arriving at the pitch. Seeing Jake, Simon, and Tony have kick about with the football, that looks way pasts its prime. There are some other player here too, including our captain, Jason, that are spread out across the pitch.

"Well, you and Kyle are always starting without us. We may as well start early ourselves," Tony says.

"Speaking of which. Where is Kyle? You two normally show up together," Simon says, looking in my direction as I near him.

"He's not coming tonight. He's catching up on work stuff." I tell them.

"Really? He's missing out on footy practice for work stuff. Again!" Jake expresses his frustration clearly.

"Exactly. It's work. It is very important stuff, you know," I tell Jake. Defending Kyle, even though he isn't here. I have noticed that it is something I have always done. Defending my best friend, and I will continue to do so. He has my back, and I have his.

"Yes, I know it's important, Mark, but we have a big game coming up soon. Against a rival team, too. We need all the practice we can get."

ON THE PITCH

"I get that, Jake. But work is work. Now c'mon guys. We can keep chatting away, or practice."

The three of them all stop for a moment after my little speech.

"He's right. C'mon lads. Let's make the most of it," Simon vocalises.

With that, the four of us rush around the pitch, passing the ball back and forth between the cones that were already set up when I arrived.

We dribble up and down the cones, working on our passes, with the goal to improve our aim with the ball, and being able to quickly pass it on to the closest player to us.

I enjoy hanging out with Jake, Tony, and Simon. Always have since I met them in school too, just like with Kyle. But it's Kyle's absence that makes me realise just how much more I enjoy playing football when he's here.

In fact, I enjoy anything and everything more when he's involved.

He's my best friend. Friends for life is what we've said to each other, and our families know that too. Everyone knows just how well we get on with each other. Kyle brings so much joy to my life. He's made me laugh when I've felt like crying. He's made me smile when I want to frown. When he smiles, it brightens my mood. He makes me feel lighter whenever I see him, every time.

He's my best friend in life, and he always will be.

"C'mon slow poke, I've seen you dribble faster than that before," Simon quips, as he receives the ball from me.

"Sorry, I was slowing down for you. You know I take it easy on players of your skill level," I joke back, and Simon playfully smirks at me.

"I think we all take it easy on Simon," Jake remarks.

"Hey, at least he didn't miss that open wide goal from five feet away," Tony mentions, much to Jake's embarrassment.

"I told you that the grass was slippery that day, and the ball was deflating, too."

"Excuses, excuses," Simon cuts in.

All four of us laugh in unison, enjoying the jokes and banter that often comes out of these practice sessions.

I like how I am treated the same as the others. Being one of the lads. But I worry that may change if they were to know that I am gay.

I realised this some time ago, and with each passing moment I spend with Jake, Tony, and Simon, and other players too, I worry more and more that they will see me differently. That they will act differently around me and will no longer treat me the same.

That is something that would hurt me.

I know I don't have to worry about Kyle changing for me. That I am confident in. I know him too well. He will remain his usual self around me, which is all I would want from anyone.

He would still be his usual soft, joyful self with me, and that is a quality I like about him.

The evening sky settles in, just as we finish.

"That was a good session, fellas. Let's keep up the momentum going for the big game," Simon vocalises with a gentle but commanding tone.

"Yeah, great works lads," Tony says. "I can see improvement from everyone."

"Cheers," Jake simply says.

ON THE PITCH

"Thanks. This really was a good session. I'm sure we will give the other team a run for their money. We won't make it easy on them at this rate," I tell them.

"You're right, Mark," Simon says.

"See you guys soon," says Tony, as he puts the cones in his car boot and is about to drive off.

"See you, Tony," I wave at him, and say bye to Jake and Simon, and drive back home.

Chapter 3
Kyle

"Something smells good, Rebecca," I say to Mark's mum upon entering her kitchen.

"Thanks, Kyle. It's my new fragrance I've been trying out, sweetie."

"Well, I was talking about your cooking, but let's go with the perfume then." I let out a soft laugh.

"I know you were," she hums and smiles back at me.

"You two get on so well together. I love it," Mark chimes in. A bright smile forms on his face. His cheeks puff out as he stands by my side.

"Yeah, you two get on *too well*. Should I be worried something is going?" Mark's dad, Peter, teases. He swiftly paces through the kitchen and pats his hand on my back.

"Oh, honey. If I were to flirt with a younger man, I wouldn't do it in front of you, nor with my son's friend." Rebecca shows Peter a mischievous smile.

"Well, that's good to hear, hun. You're still gonna flirt, but just not in front of me, or with someone I know," Peter jokingly says.

The pair of them laugh and pull each other in for a hug and a soft kiss.

"Eew, no one wants to see that," Mark says in a humorous tone, with a look of disgust on him.

"Anyway, how are you and your parents, Kyle?" Peter asks me, while turning in my direction.

"I'm good, and so are mum and dad."

"And how's the marketing agency apprenticeship going along?"

"Oh, it's going great. Best place I've ever worked. Everyone is easy to get along with, and my colleagues are fun to have a laugh with. The work itself is interesting too."

"Well, that is good to hear, Kyle. I've always said colleagues can make or break a job, regardless of the work. Having co-workers that you get along with and can have laugh together makes all the difference. Isn't that right, son?"

Peter turns his gaze to Mark.

"Yep, and I couldn't agree more," Mark replies, nodding his head as he does so. Both of them referring to their new professional connection with each other, without overtly mentioning it.

I'm happy for Mark that he got the apprenticeship he wanted. He applied for a few apprenticeships with other companies, but then his dad offered him one. I know it wasn't easy, as Peter is a one-man company, so he had to be sure he could pay Mark a wage. I think Peter also didn't possibly want to ruin anything between himself and Mark.

People often say, don't go into business with family, but I think these two will be alright. They get on so well together, and I know Mark looks up to his dad. He always comes to Peter for advice or guidance.

"You boys go sit in the conservatory. We will dish up soon, and feast," Rebecca says. "And don't worry, Kyle. I knew you were coming, so I made sure there was enough for you to."

"Thanks, Rebec," I call her by my nickname for her. "What are we having?"

"BBQ chicken wings," she answers.

"Lovely," I simply respond.

Mark and I sit on the nice wooden and modern looking chairs that are placed near the sides of the conservatory.

I always enjoy hanging out here. They have a beautiful garden, with lush green grass, with soil surrounding it with garden gnomes, too.

I remember me and Mark playing football here when we first started meeting each other after school and on weekends.

Our friendship grew so quickly. It wasn't long before both our parents become friends too. His parents came to my house, and mine to his. It's like both of our families became inseparable, just like me and him were back in school. We still are inseparable.

"So, how was practice the other day?" I ask Mark.

I couldn't make it to that session, and I know he doesn't like it when I'm not there. He doesn't explicitly say it, but he usually says something about wishing I could come, but what gives it away is his face when I tell him I can't come. He wears his emotions on his sleeve, and I always feel like shit when I cause him to be sad or disappointed.

"It was good. We've all improved. Simon even said so himself. To be honest, after finishing practice, I got confident that we can win our next game. I'm sure of it." He speaks so proudly, as he leans back on the chair, with one arm resting above the chair next to him.

ON THE PITCH

"It's good to hear that everyone's improving. I'm sure we will give the other team a run for their money. We've got the best player around here," I happily say with a nod to him.

"Oh, well, if you say so," he cheekily says. "It annoyed Jake that you couldn't make it to practice again. He became even more frustrated when I told him it was because you had work stuff going on."

"What is his problem? This isn't the first time he's taken an issue with me not showing up for practice. Which I am sorry for. I wish I could make it to every session, but I really need to meet these work deadlines and the coursework for the apprenticeship."

I look directly towards his brown eyes, hoping his response will bring me a sense of comfort. Signalling to me I haven't disappointed my best friend in the entire world. The man I know who's got my back, no matter what.

"Kyle, you don't need to apologise. I understand. You've got work stuff to finish. We're adults now. Life for us isn't like what it was back in school, where we lived carefree and had no responsibilities."

"Thanks for understanding, Mark. Talking with you has always been so easy." It always has been easy talking with him, ever since we first met.

"No problem, Kyle. Remember, if Jake or anyone else has an issue with you, let me know. I've got your back." He playfully winks at me and shows his dazzling smile.

"I know you have, Mark, and I have yours too."

I smile back at him from across the room. It's conversations and moments like this that truly make me appreciate what a wonderful friend he is, and that I am fortunate enough for him to be a part of my life.

"Here we go fellas," Peter says, as he and Rebecca walk towards the garden table from the kitchen door. Placing the plates of BBQ chicken wings in the centre, for us to gather at.

"Wow, these look great, and smell good too," says Mark.

We both sit down with Rebecca and Peter at the table.

"Thanks, sweetie," his mum says.

"Such a lovely day. Brilliant weather with good food, and splendid company. A nice day indeed," Peter says. "Cheers," he shouts, as he raises his glass of beer.

For the rest of the afternoon, I continue to enjoy the company of Mark and his parents and their warm hospitality.

It's these kinds of moments that make me remember just how close I am to Mark and his family.

It's also these moments that make me want more of Mark. Not just as friends, but as something else. Something that would bring more joy to my life but could also ruin our friendship if he ever found out how I feel.

He probably doesn't feel the same, anyway. It wasn't long ago he broke up with his ex-girlfriend Beth. So, I'm presuming he's straight.

If he were gay or bisexual, I think he would have told me by now. I'm his best friend. We tell each other everything.

Then again, I haven't told him I'm gay, but that's because of my attraction towards him.

If I didn't fancy him, I know I would have told him by now that I am gay. He would probably insist on being my wingman and trying to help me get laid by other men.

I really don't want to jeopardise our friendship by telling him how I feel. It would destroy me if that happened.

ON THE PITCH

He's my best friend. My partner in crime. He's my happiness when I am sad.

He's the light of my life.

Chapter 4
Mark

"Bye, Kyle. It was fun having you here as usual," my mum speaks up from the front door, as Kyle gets in his car.

"Thanks for the hospitality as usual, Rebecca."

"Oh, it's no problem. We love having you over."

That is true. My parents are ecstatic when Kyle hangs at our place.

"I'll see you soon, mate," I say to Kyle.

"See you too. Bye."

And with that, Kyle drives off and waves his hand out of the window.

Just as he is out of view, my younger sister, Amy, walks from around the corner of the street and paces her way to the front door.

"Hi mum," she greets.

"Hey hun. You just missed Kyle. I cooked BBQ chicken wings. I made enough for you, too."

"Thanks."

"Hi," I greet her.

"Hey." Her response is dry, and she doesn't look pleased to see me.

She's been off with me ever since I broke up with Beth. I know she was upset about that. She and Beth are close friends.

ON THE PITCH

I think what is bothering her even more is that I never gave a solid reason why I ended the relationship with Beth.

I simply told Amy and my ex, Beth, that I didn't think we were compatible anymore. Which is true.

I couldn't carry on with the relationship any longer, after realising that I am gay. It isn't ideal to be with someone when my heart pines for a man.

I had to rip the band aid off. Better to do it fast, then slowly over months or years even. That would have hurt Beth even more in the long run.

Being together for a longer duration of time would instil false beliefs of lifelong plans, like buying a house together, marriage, kids, etc.

I couldn't do that. I had to break up then, for the both of us.

Yet, I can't tell anyone the real reason I broke up with her.

At least not yet.

I would love to tell my sister the truth. Then she would stop acting so cold towards me, but if anyone in my life knew I was gay, I know they would immediately harp on me, on which man I fancy and if there is anyone, I am interested in. And I don't trust myself to hold that information in. I would cave and reveal my answer about the man I am interested in. The man who has captured my heart and put it in a cage indefinitely, has been my best friend since high school.

Kyle.

Moments later, my parents leave the house and drive to the supermarket, leaving just me and Amy together. I know she's going to want to talk about Beth. She only ever seems to bring this up when we are alone together.

"So, are you finally going to tell me why you broke Beth's heart?"

And here we go. That didn't take long.

I turn my gaze towards her, where she stands by the living room door that leads to the dining room.

"I've told you a thousand times, Amy, that Beth and I were-."

"No longer compatible. Yes, you have told me a thousand times, and you will probably continue to give me the same shitty excuse, a thousand more times, until you give me a proper answer."

Her tone is stern, with a hint of anger. I don't like it when she is like this, but I especially dislike it when she directs this tone of voice at me.

"Amy, you're my sister. I would like for us to go back to the way things were. Before you started being so cold to me and practically interrogating me whenever we're alone."

She continues to look my way, her eyes staring at mine, with her hands holding her hips on both sides.

"Well, Mark, that was a time before you broke my friend's heart for no good reason."

"YES! It was for a good reason. Now get off my case about it. The relationship was between me and Beth. So stay out of it!"

"URGH!" she groans and hastily walks away from me.

I let my frustration get the better of me. I know she's just looking out for her friend, and I get it because I'm doing the same.

If someone hurt Kyle, I would want to help him as best as I could.

But for the time being, I have to protect my reasoning why I ended the relationship. Because by keeping the real reason I broke up with Beth to myself, I'm protecting Kyle. At least that's how I see it, or maybe I'm just telling myself that.

ON THE PITCH

I want to save Kyle from any backlash or scrutiny we may face in our social circles. Especially from the people we know and meet from football.

I've heard the stories about when a team knows one of their players is gay.

It's not pretty, and Kyle is a soft soul. He's tough but I still think any negative response would get to him.

I have to protect him. He has my back and I have his. I always will. I've told him that many times, and I will stick by it until the day I die.

I'm in a bad mood now, and I know talking with Kyle will make me feel better, so I decide to text him.

Mark: Hey. Meet me at the pitch tomorrow. I could really do with talking with you. Cheers.

He quickly replies.

Kyle: Okay. I'll see you then. Take care.

I feel much better already, knowing that I am going to see Kyle tomorrow. He always makes me feel lighter.

The strain of the stress I had a moment ago, is already fading away from me. No one else has that effect on me. Only Kyle does.

Chapter 5
Kyle

"Hey," I softly greet Mark, making my way to him in the centre of the pitch.

"Hi," he simply says.

Something's up with him. I can tell. He may be all smiles at me, but I've known him long enough to know when something is bothering him, and I can tell right away as soon as he opened his mouth.

"Mark, what's up?"

"Wow, you really know me so well, or was it that obvious?"

"Not obvious. I really know you like the back of my hand," I tell him.

"If you're referring to your right hand, then that is an accomplishment. Since I know that's your wanking hand."

"W-what?" I almost choke on my own words.

He slowly smirks at me with joy.

"I was not expecting you to say that."

"Well, you know me so well, Kyle. Something is bothering me. My sister Amy."

"Ah," I simply let out.

Mark has mentioned to me before how Amy has been a pain in the ass ever since he broke up with Beth.

ON THE PITCH

It surprised me he broke up with her, when he first mentioned it to me, here at the pitch, a day before he ended the relationship.

He seemed distressed back then. Had been for a while up to that point. But once he spoke with Beth, he seemed to be back to his usual self. He seemed lighter.

I remember being annoyed and upset with myself, that I couldn't help him out when he spoke to me on that day.

I've always helped when I can. I don't enjoy seeing him distressed. It pains me to see him like that. I wanted to help, but it felt like he wasn't letting me in. Which hurt, as it felt like he was shutting me out.

But I know him well. If he didn't want to tell me too much, he had would have had his reasons.

"Here come the others," Mark says, and I turn around to see Jake, Tony, and Simon pacing themselves towards us.

"Did you knew they were coming?"

"I did, but only found out an hour ago. Good thing we still got to have our one-to-one conversation. I'm glad we have these kinds of talks with each other. I don't think I could talk about stuff like this with the other lads," Mark informs me.

"Yeah, same. You're the only person I do have these deep talks with."

I meet his gaze quickly before the others reach us.

"I'm glad you're my best friend, Mark. I wouldn't know what I would do without you."

He lingers into my eyes, with those ocean beautiful brown eyes of his.

"Right back at you, Kyle." He reaches his arm out and rests his hand on my shoulder. "You've been a good friend to me. Now, let's go play and smash this."

A wide smile forms on his face.

"Lets."

We both meet the others halfway, meeting them in the middle of the pitch.

"Hey boys," I greet them all at once.

"Yay, it's good to see you, Kyle," says Simon. He places a ball on the ground and holds it still with his boot.

"Yeah, you actually showed up for once," Jake snaps at me.

"That's enough, Jake." Mark says in a sharp tone. Having my back as usual.

"Yeah, come on, Jake. Kyle had work that day. We're adults now, with adult responsibilities." Tony also chimes in.

"Fine. Let's just play," Jake begrudgingly says.

I quickly glance over to Mark, and he winks back at me, while also showing me his signature smile.

Simon kicks the ball in the middle of all of us, and we all quickly scatter around the pitch, passing the ball from one another. I know they were practicing their passes in the last session, so I am glad I can catch up with the rest now.

I claim possession of the ball and dribble my way over to the other side of the pitch. The green of the grass fades into a blur as I quickly glance down to the ball in front of me when I hear Tony shout from my left.

"Kyle, over here."

ON THE PITCH

Quickly, I turn just a smidge in his direction, and with my right leg, I kick the ball over to him, covering at least ten feet.

"Nice pass," I hear Simon praise me.

"Thanks, Simon."

Seconds later, Simon rushes to the other side and passes the ball to Jake, who then passes it on to Tony.

Mark runs closer to the goal that is near Tony.

"Tony, pass it here," Mark shouts.

With a quick play by Tony, he jolts the ball over to Mark, who then wallops the ball into the goal, from about fifteen feet.

"Great shot, Mark!" I congratulate him.

"Keep shooting goals like that, and we'll be giving other teams some trouble, that's for sure." Jake says, as he slowly eases from running into walking.

Another half an hour passes by, and we call it quits for the evening.

"Keep up the good work, fellas. We're all making progress. I can see improvement from everyone," Tony compliments. He's always acted like a coach to us. I've said to him previously that I think he would make for an excellent coach.

"Cheers Tony," Mark says, as he pats Tony on the back.

Mark and I stay behind at the pitch while the others leave.

We wave them off as they leave the parking lot.

I walk side by side with Mark. We make our way to the bench area.

We sit ourselves down, and simply enjoy the silence that now surrounds us, after a fast-paced game of footy.

We look up towards the late spring sun, slowly settling away, ready for the night sky to take over.

"It's beautiful," Mark states.

"It sure is."

Both of us breathe out deeply. Catching some air as we rest.

"Mark."

"Yeah?" He slightly turns his head towards me, but not all the way.

"What are you going to do about Amy?"

He turns his head back to its original position. Facing across the pitch in front of us.

"I'm not sure, man. I don't know how to fix this."

He looks down beneath the bench, and damn, I wish I could help him so badly. But how can I, if he himself doesn't know how to fix this? It's his sister, after all. He would know what to do better than me.

"I'm sure with time, all things will turn out well. You just got to have hope, even when you don't know what to do." He says in a tone that is very unusual for him to speak with.

Another moment of silence passes between us, and the sky has become slightly dimmer than what it was when we sat down.

"Kyle." He softly calls my name, while we both still continue to look out across the pitch.

"Yeah?"

"I... I'm..."

He swallows on his next word, cutting off whatever he was about to say next.

"Are you okay, Mark?"

"I am Kyle. It's just some things are difficult to say. You know what I mean?"

"I know that," I tell him in a calming tone.

ON THE PITCH

I know that very well, Mark. Is what I would like to tell him. But I'm not ready yet to tell him I'm gay.

But fuck, this is such a suitable moment to tell him. It's just the two of us out here, on the pitch. A place where we have spoken many times one-to-one. Just like we did earlier, before the others showed up.

This is a place where we have confided in each other. Shared our secrets, our troubles. Worn our hearts on our sleeves for the other to see.

Yet, I can't do that right now. I don't want to complicate his life anymore right now.

Because I don't trust myself not to hold back on who has claimed my heart. The man I love and have done so for the longest time.

The man I enjoy spending as much time with as possible.

The man who makes my heart flutter when I see a text notification from him.

The man I want to wake up in the morning with his arms around me.

That man has and always will be my best friend.

"Kyle. Thanks for always being there for me. You're a good friend."

"Sure thing. I will always be there for you, Mark. You know that."

I smile brightly at him as he turns around to face me.

"Yeah, I know that." He smiles back.

"Look, man. I'm sorry for not speaking much. It's just... well, Amy's on my mind and other stuff, too."

His smile fades away, and a look of sadness takes over.

"It's alright. Besides, it was great just sitting with you here, enjoying the quietness. Looking at the sky as the sun fades."

"Yeah, this has been nice," he says. "I'm gonna get off now. Will talk another time."

He reaches his arm out, starting a fist bump.

I do the same and our fists touch while we both softly smile at one another.

"Take care, Mark. I'll see you soon."

"See you, Kyle."

And with that, we part ways for the day and head back to our homes.

Chapter 6
Kyle

I texted Sarah, my other best friend, one who I don't secretly love, that I want to meet up and speak with her.

I can't tell Mark about my feelings for him, but I know I can talk to Sarah about this.

She already knows that I am gay. She's the only person who knows right now.

I am fortunate enough to know that my parents wouldn't have any negative response when they find out, but I know that once I tell them, it will for sure get back to Mark, and I'm not ready for that. At least not yet.

I pull outside her house, that she recently moved into. I think she's the only person in my group of friends that now have their own place.

I reach the door and press on the doorbell.

I can hear the double-chime sounds from within, signalling my arrival.

"Hey, come on in," she says, after she pulls the door open.

"Hi Sarah." I step inside her home, and immediately I pick up the scent of lavender wax melt candles.

"You and these wax melts. You're obsessed with them."

"Well, some of them you bought me for my birthday, so don't complain," she claps back.

"Good point," I tell her, whilst I place my bomber jacket on her coat hanger.

"Go make yourself comfortable in the back garden. It's a lovely day and I've got the patio door open. I'll make us both a brew," she informs me.

"Ooh, look at you. With your own place, and a patio too."

"You'll get your own place eventually," she tells me. "All within due time," she concludes.

I cut through the patio door and rest by the garden table. Once settled, I adjust my position to ensure the parasol in the centre of the table protects my eyes from the sun. I already squint my eyes enough.

A moment later and Sarah walks towards me with two mugs. Coffee for me, and tea for her.

"Here you go," she places my mug on the table, and sits on the chair that is placed on the side of the table, towards my left.

We both take a sip of our drinks, and just take in the moment. The calm warm breeze gently grazing our exposed arms. The sun in the mostly clear blue skies. We both let out a sigh before we begin the heavy conversation.

"So, Kyle. What's on your mind?"

She turns her body slightly towards me, taking off her sunglasses now that her face is under the shade from the parasol.

"Straight to the point, as usual with you."

"You know it," she smiles.

"Sarah, I think it's time I come out to my parents."

Her jaw slightly drops right before she takes another sip of tea.

ON THE PITCH

"Good. I'm happy for you. You and I both know that your parents will still accept you as you are."

I take another sip of my coffee and let her words sink in for what they are. The truth.

"I know that. It's just... well." I lose track of my thoughts.

I take in a deep breath and look out towards her beautiful garden.

"It's just I don't know how to tell them without making it out like a big thing. So, I was wondering if you could be there with me when I come out to them."

"Sure, of course I will. But won't me coming make this into a 'big thing?"

She has a point.

"Yeah, but you being there would make it less nerve racking for me, then if I were to do it alone."

"Understood," she says. "I would be more than happy to do this for you. When do you plan on telling them?"

"Tomorrow. After work. Is that alright with your schedule?"

"Yes, it is," she answers.

"Thanks Sarah. I knew I could count on you."

"As always." She cracks a smile, and downs a big sip from her mug, and places it back on the table. "But go on, I know there's more you're not telling me, Kyle."

"Damn, you're fucking good."

"Thanks, but in all seriousness, Kyle. You don't have to say anything more if you don't want to."

"I know Sarah."

She's always been considerate like that, ever since we first met when my parents moved to Huyton, and she became one of my neighbours.

"Well, there is something else, Sarah. I know it has puzzled you why I haven't yet told my parents about me being gay, and that's because there is someone close to me who I don't want to potentially ruin my relationship with them if they knew. I worry that the more people know, the more likely it is that this person will find out."

Sarah takes a moment to digest what I have just told her. Presumably trying to make sense of my words.

"Well, couldn't you just tell your parents, not to tell this person that you are gay?"

"I could, and I have thought of that. But they, especially my mum, would just badger me to spill the details, and I think I would cave," I tell her.

"What is it exactly, that you don't want this other person in your life to know about it?"

"Well, this person will probably know at some point, but for the time being, I'm not ready for them to know."

"Is it because you're attracted to this person?"

She figures me out so easily.

"Yes, it is," I reveal.

"Okay. This makes more sense to me now."

She takes one more sip of her tea. Leaving the mug empty and warm on the table.

I take one last sip of coffee too and place my mug next to hers.

"Kyle. Are you fine with me taking a guess who I think this person is?"

I take a moment to contemplate whether I want to know her answer. Ultimately, I realise that if someone was going to guess correctly, it would be Sarah. So, I may as well rip the band aid off.

ON THE PITCH

"Sure. Go ahead."

"It's Mark, isn't it?"

"Yup. You are correct."

I knew she would be. No doubt in my mind that she wouldn't have picked someone else.

"What made you think it was, Mark?" I ask of her.

"Oh, come on. It was easy to pick up on. Besides, you two are extremely close. You always have been ever since you met each other. You're practically inseparable. The both of you get on so well together."

"That's what everyone tells us."

"Oh, my. Now that I've got the image of you two together, I can't get it out of my head. You two would make for a cute couple."

"Now you're getting obsessed over us," I joke.

"Oh my god, we have to come up with a ship name. Erm…"

She's rambling on now, and it's adorable when she gets like this.

"What about Kyark?"

"Nah," I tell her, and her face says the same.

"Yeah, I'm not a fan of it once I said it. Ooh, how about Kylark?"

"That one sounds better," I answer.

"Yeah, it does. Ok, so Kylark it is."

"Ha, well, we don't even know if Mark is gay or bisexual. So, all of my worries could be for nothing."

"You'll never know if you don't ask or open up to him."

I take another deep breath and take in what Sarah just told me. She's right. I know she is.

I should be able to tell Mark how I feel. I always do, but with this, I'm not sure.

I don't want to lose my best friend. I just wish that I knew that no matter what I say to him, we will remain the best of friends.

But I'm afraid of the possibility of losing him. I can't bear the thought of that happening. He's the light of my life, and I just wish he knew that.

"Sarah. Thanks for the talk and for agreeing to be with me when I tell my parents. You're always so helpful."

"No problem. Just text me when you're ready and I'll be there."

"Will do."

We go back inside her house, and I pick up my jacket.

"I'll see you tomorrow," I say.

"Yeah, see you tomorrow. And Kyle?"

"Yes?"

"Try not to be too nervous."

"I'll try," I tell her and go in for a hug.

She opens the door for me, and I head out.

"Bye Sarah."

"Bye Kyle."

I drive back home. Ready and prepared for tomorrow.

Chapter 7
Mark

"How much longer do you think this job will take, dad?"

"Erm... I'd say about another hour at least."

"Okay then."

I'm at another house with my dad, working on someone's broken kitchen sink. Part of my plumbing apprenticeship.

I enjoy working with my dad. It's been a blast.

In the end, I am glad I am working with him, instead of doing my apprenticeship with another business, and possibly working eight hours a day with some crappy boss and co-workers.

This is much better

"Why do you ask? Not in a rush, are you?"

"No. I was just curious. It just feels like this job is taking longer than expected. We've done jobs like this before, and they were over by now."

"Not every kitchen sink is the same, and not all issues are the same. We don't want to rush the job and risk getting a shitty review online."

"That is true," is all I say.

He's laying down on his back, with his head in the sink cupboards.

I watch everything as he works. Even the smallest of details.

I want to learn all I can, so that I can be just as a competent of a plumber as my dad.

My goal being to one day be self-employed with my own work van. Working on my time.

I need to be out and about, working with my hands. There is no way I could work in an office. I've known that for a long time. Company meetings, video calls, spreadsheets, and a stuffy cubicle. All of it sounds absolutely awful to me. I don't know how Kyle can enjoy that environment so much. But different strokes, for different folks.

"Pass me that, son." My dad points to the wrench by the toolbox that is near the bottom of his legs.

"Sure. Here you go." I pass it to him, and he tightens it around the pipe underneath the sink.

I can't wait to get a shower when I get home. My clothes smell from all the work we've done today. Thankfully, this is the last job for the rest of the day. My work shirt and trousers desperately need cleaning, too.

"Son. Are you alright?"

"Yeah, I am. Why do you ask?"

I know why he's probably asked. Still, I'm surprised he's asking me this.

"Well, I heard about the little spat you and your sister got into. She's still upset with you for breaking up with Beth."

"Yeah, I know," I reply with a sarcastic tone.

"I'm still not sure why you broke with her. She's a sweet girl, and it seemed like you two got on perfectly fine."

"We got along at first, but by the end, we just didn't."

I may not be telling my father the whole reason I split up with her, but what I told him was true.

ON THE PITCH

Me and Beth just didn't click as we once used to. Though, maybe that was because my mind and heart were no longer in it.

"There has to be more to it than that," he says.

"Well, there isn't." There sure is, dad. I just don't want to tell you, or anyone else. At least not yet.

"Me and Beth were just no longer-."

"Compatible," he finishes my sentence.

He tilts his head towards me. Showing me his wide grin.

"Clearly you've spoken to Amy about this."

"Not so much speaking to her. More like she just loudly retells the conversation you two had. Over and over."

"Do you think she'll get over it?" I ask him.

"With time, yes. I'm sure. Plus, when she gets into a relationship herself, I'm sure she'll understand."

I know what he means. Amy had a boyfriend briefly when she was seventeen, but they weren't too serious. Me and Beth were together for a year and a half. At a later age too, when we were both twenty-one.

"I hope so. I don't like it when she's being like this with me."

"You're siblings. Siblings squabble."

He pulls himself out from underneath the sink and places the wrench back in the toolbox.

"That's it. We're done here, and for the rest of the day. You go put everything back in the van. I'll collect payment from Mrs Anderson and tell her we're done."

"Okay then."

I slide the van door open and store all the tools back inside it. It's a typical white workers' van, but with my dad's name and contact details on the side of it.

I wait inside the van, sitting on the passenger seat. Ready for my dad to come out of the house.

Kyle isn't the only one I am worried about when I come out. My dad's reaction to it is also on my mind.

I know nothing negative will come from it, which I am fortunate to say.

I just worry that he will act differently around me. That he won't be his usual self.

He's a soft man, but he does come from a blue-collar background, where men are supposed to be 'men'.

Though I should give him more credit. He has often mentioned how he hated growing up in that environment, and always pushed back against it.

I remember my mum telling me that was something she admired about him when they first started dating. That he wasn't the usual stoic, silent man. But light-hearted and easy-going.

Damn, I don't know what to do.

"Okay, take care, and if there's any more issues, just call me," my dad says to Mrs Anderson, as leaves her house and walks towards the van.

"Another job done and another working day over with," he cheerfully says upon returning to the driver's seat.

He puts the key in the ignition, and before he switches it on, I suddenly reconsider my stance on telling him.

"Dad, I'm gay."

A drop of silence falls on us. My heartbeat picks up.

I'm nervous. I just want him to say something.

"Dad, say some-."

ON THE PITCH

"You're still my son, Mark." He cuts me off, but I don't mind it at all.

"Gay, straight, or something else, you're my son. I care for you all the same. No matter what."

He shows me his warm, welcoming smile. Seeing it makes me feel much better.

"Thanks dad. That means a lot to me."

"Does your mother know?"

"No. Not yet."

"Do you want me to be there when you tell her?"

"Yes, I would like that."

"No problem," he says, and he pulls me in for a warm hug.

"So, you have the missing piece of the puzzle now," I tell him, and he looks puzzled himself. "The breakup. This was the main reason I broke up with Beth. I realised I was gay."

"Ohhh." He looks like he is mentally putting all the pieces together.

"So, you realised this about yourself, once you were already with her?"

"Yes."

"Ah. Alright. It makes sense. You two got together at a young age. A time when you're still figuring things out."

"Dad, I'm still trying to figure things out."

"And it never stops. Not even at my age," he laughs, and so do I.

I feel much lighter now that I've told someone, but especially him. He's been my hero ever since I was a child. Mum always told me I was a daddy's boy when growing up.

"Oh, before we go. I got something for you. It's from Mrs Anderson."

He hands me a ten-pound note.

"A tenner? Nice."

"She said you were a hard worker and put a lot of effort in. She even said that I should be proud of you. I told her I already am."

"Okay dad, now you're just being cheesy."

We both let out a small laugh again, and he turns the engine on.

"Come on. Let's go back home," he says.

We drive back home, and I feel much happier than I did earlier on.

Having this moment with my dad has left me feeling more confident. Confidence which I could have used yesterday, when it was just me and Kyle left on the bench, after football practice.

I still can't believe I almost told him I was gay, right at that moment.

But that is for another time.

Chapter 8
Kyle

"Hi. I'm glad you came." I welcome Sarah, just as she walks up to my house.

I saw her park outside. I've been waiting to see her pull up from my couch, for what feels like ages, but really only like twenty minutes.

"Hey," she whispers. "How are you?"

"Nervous, but better now that you're here."

She smiles brightly at that. We have always been there for each other, and I'm glad we have remained friends ever since we first met.

"Come on in. My parents are out in the back."

We make our way through the living room and out to the back garden to meet my parents.

"Mum. Dad. Sarah's here."

"Sarah, so lovely to see you," my mum welcomes her.

"Hi Sarah. How's your new home coming along?" My dad asks her.

"It's going well. I have decorated most of the house. I just have a few bits and bobs to sort out."

"It's great when you finally have your own place." My mum tells her.

"Yeah, me and her, we're thrilled we could get it on without disturbing no one."

"Eew dad. Too much information," I vocalise with a hint of repulse to my tone.

"Hey, if it weren't for us moving out and making the most of it, you wouldn't have been born." He laughs, with a big grin on his face.

"Okay, hun. Can we not talk about our sex lives in front of our son and Sarah?" My mum says with a humorous tone.

A few more seconds go by, and along with it, so does the fun-laid back atmosphere.

I think they can both sense something is up.

"Mum. Dad. I'd like to talk to you both. Can we sit at the table?"

I wave my hand, motioning them towards the garden table that is placed near to the patio door behind me.

"Sure thing," my mum says with a worried look on her face.

"Don't worry. It's nothing bad. No medical or financial issues, or whatever you think it is."

That seems to have eased some worries from them both. Especially my mum. Her worried facial expression from a moment ago, isn't there now. But I know her. She will still think of the worst news imaginable in her head.

Mum, dad, and I sit down first at the table. Sarah joins us a couple of seconds later and she sits right beside me.

Dad and mum quickly glance over at each other, as Sarah sat down. I notice they now look concerned again.

I swallow hard and speak.

"Mum. Dad. There is something I want to tell you, and I have been holding off on telling you for some time now. But thanks to Sarah here." She reaches her hand out and holds onto mine. "I feel ready to tell you."

"Mum. Dad. I-."

"Oh, my god. You've got her pregnant. Haven't you?" My mum shouts.

"What! No."

"But you two are friends. When did you two get together?" My dad questions myself and Sarah.

I notice Sarah has turned pale and is completely shocked, just like me.

"You two aren't ready to have a baby. You don't even have your own place. And Kyle, you haven't even finished your marketing apprenticeship yet," my mum rambles on.

"I don't know when you two became a thing, but it would have been wise to wait until you're both settled into your careers before such a big change. How are you-."

"Mum, I'm gay."

Silence fills the gap between us. Their facial expressions have remained stiff since I spoke.

"Well, that certainly got you to shut up," I say jokingly. Showing them a playful smile.

"Oh," is all my dad lets out.

"So, you're not pregnant then, Sarah?" My mum questions.

"Nope. I'm not. But if I were, you don't have to worry about Kyle being the father." She chuckles.

"Woo. Thank God. Panic over," my mum says, as she leans back in her chair. Taking a deep breath.

"You two had us worried there for a sec," dad says. Smiling in relief.

"What made you two think I had got her pregnant?"

"Well, you said you had something to tell us, and she was next to you, holding your hand. It looked like you both had something to tell us," mum states.

"Oh, yeah. When you put it like that, I can see how you thought that."

"Ha-ha. Wow. Ha." Sarah bursts into a fit of laugher.

"What's so funny?" I ask her.

"It's just that... I can't believe they really thought we had sex." Her laugh continues to escape her mouth as she tries to smile. Sarah then glances back at my parents. "Like, your son is good looking and very handsome, but imagine us being a thing? Like he is not my type, and as you now know. I am definitely not his type." She gleefully smiles again.

Judging from the looks of my mum and dad, they seemed to have taken in what I have just told them, and I notice my mum's lips curl into a smile.

"We still love you. I hope you weren't worried that would change," my mother says.

"Oh, no. I knew nothing bad would come from you two. That I am thankful for. But I was still nervous to tell you both, so I had already told Sarah previously, and asked her to be here for me today. I'm glad she came."

I turn back and smile at Sarah. Showing my appreciation for her support.

"Come here son," dad says, and he pulls me in for a hug. "Just like your mum said. We still love you and that will never change."

"I know, dad." I hold on to the hug for a second longer, and he sits back down.

ON THE PITCH

"So, which celeb do you fancy?" My mum asks me.

"Oof... erm, I'd have to say Luke Evans. He is fit."

"Oh, he absolutely is," Sarah interjects.

"I can't picture him. What's he in?" Mum asks and Sarah looks him up online on her phone and shows a picture of him to my mum.

"Oh, him? Oh yes. He is gorgeous." My mum blushes, teasing dad as she does so.

"Oh boy. Look what you two have started. Now she won't stop gushing over him," my dad jokes.

"You're right hun," my mum tells him.

All four of us continue to stay outside in the back garden. Soaking in the sun and enjoying each other's company.

I'm glad I've told my parents now. I feel so much better because of it. But the other most important person in my life still doesn't know, and that hurts. Because I want to be open with Mark with every part of me.

But telling him will mean opening the door to him even more. I know I would desire more from him and I'm not even sure if he feels the same way.

Whatever happens, I just hope I don't lose my best friend.

Chapter 9
Mark

"Dad said you wanted to talk, mum?" I vocalise my question as I enter the kitchen and see mum, dad, and Amy gathered at the table.

I sit opposite them, waiting for one of them to speak.

"Your dad here has told us the news about you," my mum reveals.

I'm not mad. I had told dad on our way back home that he can tell the rest of the household about me. Speaking to him one to one in the van was emotionally draining, and I did not want to have to do that all over again.

"Thanks," I quietly say to dad, with a gentle nod of the head to him. He shows me a warm smile in response.

"Mark, I'm so sorry," Amy blurts out with an apologetic tone. A sad look washes over her.

"I'm sorry for giving you a hard time about breaking up with Beth. I have been a right bitch towards you," she lightly chuckles. "Even though I now know the real reason you broke up with her, I still should never have treated you like I did. Just like you told me, the relationship was between you two, and I should never have been pestering you about it. Again, I'm sorry."

ON THE PITCH

Hearing her say those two words suddenly washes away all the stress I've had for these past few days since our last argument. I feel calmer and at ease already.

"Apology accepted."

I get off my chair and go to her hug. "Yay, I got my loveable sister back," I tease.

"Hey, I'm always lovable."

"No, you're bloody not," my dad cuts in with his unique humorous tone.

"Mum. Aren't you going to defend my honour?" Amy says.

"Well, I would, sweetie, but it's hard to do so when they're speaking the truth." A growing smirk forms on my mum's face.

"Woah, she's got you there sis," I playfully tease.

Our mum swoops both me and Amy with her arms. Pulling us in for one big hug.

"All that matters is that my children have made up and are back on speaking terms," my mum cheerfully says.

"Yeah, for now at least," my dad chimes in.

"Just let me have this moment of peacefulness while it lasts," my mum tells him.

This is something I will always cherish. Moments like these that will become pleasant memories to look back on.

Life is short, and it's moments such as this that make me grateful for the people in my life. Family, friends. They all make life worth living.

Chapter 10
Kyle

It has been a couple of days since I spent time with my parents and Sarah in our back garden, and I've felt lighter than air ever since I spoke with them. It truly feels like a weight has been lifted off my shoulders, and the sunny warm weather just keeps on adding to my joyful state of mind. The perfect weather for some football practice.

It thrilled me earlier this morning when I noticed a text from Mark asking to meet him at the pitch.

It's been a few days since I last saw him. It was a nice and calm moment with him, looking at the sunset while we sat on the bench at the pitch.

Though he seemed... off. I couldn't quite figure out what was up with him. Heck, I still don't, but I hope he's fine now.

"Hey, Kyle."

I turn around and see Mark approaching me. The warm summer breeze gently pushes through his shorts and team shirt.

His lips slowly form into a dashing smile with each step he takes towards me.

"Hi, Mark. How are you?"

I pull him in for a hug. The hug that friends do, by patting one another on the back. But if only I could hug him differently. A way that brings me closer to him.

"I'm fine. In fact, I'm fucking great," he says, so full of cheer and pride.

"Wow. Well, tell me then. Why are you in such a good mood?"

"Because Kyle. I've told my family something about myself and it felt so good and uplifting when I told. In fact, what I told them, I was about to tell you the last time we sat here on this bench."

Quickly, I feel my stomach drop. I think I know what he's about to say next. I feel my palms begin to sweat and shake in anticipation of what Mark is going to say.

He locks onto my eyes with his beautiful brown eyes, and he slowly takes in a deep breath. "Kyle. I'm gay."

"Me too," I quickly say, with not even a second after him.

"W-what?" His jaw drops and his bottom lip trembles.

"How long have you known for?" He asks, as his face is still showing his shock at my response.

"Erm... I'm not too sure. I think I've known for probably a couple of years, but I think lately my feelings on the matter have become too strong. My feelings went from having a casual attraction to men I see in public and celebs to romantic feelings. Oh, and also being really fucking horny. I have fantasised so much about hot, shirtless men."

"Ha, me too," he adds.

Mark places himself on the bench, and I follow suit and sit right beside him. Just like we did the last time we were here, but now watching the morning sunrise instead of sunset.

"What about gay porn? Have you watched some?"

I roll my eyes and give my answer. "Oh, loads Mark. Absolutely loads. So much of it."

"I figured that. You horny bastard."

I gently fist bump his shoulder and smirk at him.

"Come on. I know you've probably watched some too," I say.

"I have, but still probably not as much as you." Mark turns to me and chuckles. I look into his soul piercing eyes as he turns to look back toward the sunrise.

"What celebs do you fancy?" I ask him.

"Ooh, where do I begin? Tom Hardy, Luke Evans, Daniel Craig and who else. Oh and Idris Elba."

"Keeping your taste at home, then. All of those are British."

"Oh yeah. I hadn't realised that until you said it."

He lets out another light chuckle. It's cute when he does it. I've always enjoyed hearing it for as long as I have known him.

"Now it's your turn. Which celebs tickle your fancy?"

"Tom Hardy and Luke Evans too. I also like Tom Daley and Channing Tatum," I answer.

"Channing Tatum? You're such a basic gay."

"I don't care. I just know that if he were running on this pitch now, shirtless, I would not take my eyes off him."

We both cackle with laughter while we both turn to look back at each other. I'm so glad that I am now completely open with him about who I am, and I am so happy that he is now open with his family and myself.

"Wait, a sec. I have just realised something. When I said I was gay, you immediately said, *'me too.'* Did you know what I was about to say?" He questions, with his eyes concentrating on mine.

ON THE PITCH

"Well, once you said that you were about to tell me the last time we were here, I had a hunch, along with how you were speaking."

"Fair enough. That makes sense." He simply responds.

"I'm glad you told me," I say softly and gently hold on to his shoulder. Letting him know I am here for him.

"Yeah, I'm glad I did too, and that you did as well."

He leans his head on my rested hand. Nudging into his shoulder. It's odd. We've been close like this for a long time, but we're friends. Yet, if someone walked by and saw us, they would think we were a couple.

"It's good to have a close friend you can rely on and count on for support." He calmly speaks with a warm and relaxing tone.

"It sure is, Mark. I'm glad we've got each other. I wouldn't know what I would do without you, mate."

"Same. Anyway. Let's have a kick about. Just you and me. Like old times."

"Great. I've missed our one-to-one sessions."

It has been a long time since me and Mark have had our own little games. The two of us dribbling the ball and shooting for goals. Yeah, sure, it may not be the best method of practice when we haven't got our other team members with us, but that isn't the point of these sessions. It's all about me and Mark, having fun and connecting with one another. It's during moments like this in the past, where we have bonded more and opened up to each other. That has never happened with the other players. Only with Mark. Only with him I feel I could be my true self and let my guard down. I believe our one-to-one football sessions sped up our friendship.

Mark raises himself off the bench and grabs the ball out of his bag and quickly kicks it into the centre of the pitch.

"Come on," he shouts as he runs towards the ball.

I quickly catch up to him and dash for the ball, kicking it further away from him and follow it up.

"Oh, no you don't Preston," he calls out.

"Woah, using my surname, are you?" I shout and dribble the ball away from him. The grass becomes a blur with the speed I am going at.

"Yes, I am, and I am not letting you get the first goal."

He quickly catches up to me and slides his leg to the ball. Darting it across the pitch.

"Fuck," I shout. "You ain't winning, Thomas," I call him by his surname.

"You haven't called me by that for a very long time," he says but just barely, as he picks up the pace towards the goal.

I make a mad dash for it and run aggressively towards my side of the pitch.

He's already kicked the ball, so my opportunity to tackle it away from him has gone.

I run in front of the goal post and stretch my hand out, trying to block the ball as it swings through the air, nearing closer to me.

I stretch my fingers out perfectly straight, hoping that I can still block the ball, but it doesn't happen. The ball swerves past me and hits the net.

"YES! GOAL!" Mark triumphantly shouts.

ON THE PITCH

"Shit. Now I won't hear the end of this for some time," I say to him. Looking at him and seeing his shit-eating grin. A grin I've become all too familiar with over the years.

"You're right about that, Preston." He charmingly smirks at me and goes to shake my hand.

"Still last naming me, hey." I shake his hand. "I'll win the next game between us."

"I'm sure you said that last time when it was just us and, well, here we are. Me, the winner. Yet again."

"Ugh, cocky Mark, is back. No one likes cocky Mark. I will warn your parents and Amy about this."

"Shut up," he says playfully and lightly fist bumps me on my chest. He is still showing his warm smile.

Fuck, Mark. If only you knew how badly I want to kiss that smile of yours right now.

"This has been fun, Mark. We should do this more often. Just us two out here on the pitch."

"For sure. It has been so long since we last did this."

We both head back to the bench and pack up our belongings.

"Are you busy this Saturday, Mark?"

"No. Why?" he says to me.

"Well, you haven't been to my house for a while and my parent miss you. You know how much they love you. They're making dinner and asked me to invite you. So, can you come?"

"Yeah sure. I'll be there. I miss their hospitality. Every time I come to yours, I get treated like a king."

"I know. You get treated better than me sometimes, and I'm their son. I swear if they could, they'd swap me for you."

"Ha, I've joked the same thing about you with my parents. They always ask me when you will next pop round."

With our items now packed in our bags, we both walk back to our cars that are parked in the parking lot by the pitch.

"Kyle. Today was a good day. I'm glad we can both be fully open with each other." Mark tells me just as we stop in our tracks by the car park.

"Today has been amazing and yeah, I'm happy too, Mark. I'll see you on Saturday."

I pat him on the shoulder and turn to my car door.

"I will see you then. Bye, Kyle," he says and waves at me.

"Bye, Mark." I wave back at him, and with that, we both turn on our ignitions and drive out of the car park.

Chapter 11
Mark

As I lay here in my bed, staring at the ceiling after waking up, the first thought that pops in my head is that I wonder if Kyle finds me attractive.

I reflect on some of our recent interactions, and nothing is jumping out to me that would indicate he finds me attractive.

Well, come to think of it. I know he thinks I'm good looking. He's said so before. I remember him saying to Beth that she scored well when me and her got together.

"Aye," I sigh out loud to myself in my bedroom.

It's great to know that Kyle is gay, because at least I can now turn to my best friend for when I want to discuss gay related topics and fawn over the men that we find attractive like we did yesterday on the bench at the pitch.

But man, knowing he is gay *and* that I want him more than just as a friend, has left me feeling odd ever since I got home after practice with him.

I hope he feels the same way. I want to know if he does. Heck, I need to know. The feeling of not knowing is clawing away at me.

After wallowing in my thoughts, I decide to jump out of bed and head down towards the kitchen.

"Morning dad," I greet him upon entering. I quickly scrummage through the cupboards and decide to have some cereal for breakfast.

"Morning son. Are you excited about the big game? It's coming up soon."

"I sure am. I can't wait to smash the other team," I say with a prideful tone.

"Oh. You seem confident that you will win?"

"I am. Do you not think we can win this?" I raise my brow at him.

"I think you can, but that's just me speaking as your dad. I have to say that. Part of being a parent. Telling your kids that you believe in them, and they can accomplish anything they want. You know. Giving them false hope." He smiles across from the table as I sit down with my bowel of cereal.

"Oh, well, thanks for the confidence, dad," I sarcastically say.

"No problem." He laughs for a couple of seconds.

He's always making everyone laugh first thing in the morning. I think he does it to set a bright and cheerful mood for everyone before we all go about on our day.

"Morning," my mum greets the both of us upon entering.

"Morning mum."

"Morning lovely," my father says, "Hun, do you think Mark and the boys will win this big game?"

"Of course I do," my mum says so innocently.

"Yeah, but we just say that because we're his parents. Don't we?"

"Well, of course. It would be horrible if we said we didn't believe he could win."

"And thanks to you too mum, for the false confidence."

ON THE PITCH

"Fine. For the next game after this one, I will say I think you and the boys are shit and there ain't no way you can win. Is that better?" She raises her brow and shows her soft smile to us.

"It would be the same to me either way," I reply.

"It would be the truth," says my dad.

"Peter!" My mum lightly slaps him with the tea towel.

My dad just giggles with an infectious laugh.

"O... kay. What's going on here?" Amy says by the kitchen door.

"Long story," my mother tells her.

Amy grabs a bowel of the same cereal I am having and sits by me. It's wonderful that we're back on speaking terms. I missed her pleasant company.

"Hey," she quietly says and shows me a warm smile.

"Hey to you too," I gently nudge to her.

"Awe, this is so sweet to see," my mum gushes.

"Ugh, okay mum. Get over it," Amy says, looking a little embarrassed.

"Fine," my mum scoffs. "Mark, I heard that you're going to Kyle's tomorrow for dinner with him and his parents. That sounds nice."

"Yes, I am. I'm looking forward to it. How did you find out?" I question my mother.

"Sam told me."

My mum and Kyle's mum often speak over the phone. I should have guessed that's how she knew.

Suddenly, my mum and Amy are both staring at me. Their eyes locked onto me like a vulture stalking its prey.

"What's with the dagger eyes, you two?"

"Well, it's just that you're going to Kyle's tomorrow and, well, you know?" My mother coyly says, with a mischievous look on her.

"Know what?" I question.

"We know Kyle is also gay and now you're going to his place when you haven't been there for a while. The timing is suspicious," Amy interjects. Getting her words out quick and fast.

"What do you mean by suspicious?"

"Well, you both came out around the same time, and now you're going to his place," Amy says.

My dad has now left the kitchen. I wish I could so that I can escape this conversation, but mum and Amy would only follow me.

"You know nothing is happening between us, and Sam and Ben are going to be there. So if something were to happen between me and Kyle, we wouldn't do anything with his parents nearby."

That seems to appease them both, for now at least.

"Fair point," my mum says. "But do you think he's good looking?"

"Of course I do. He's a good-looking man," I answer.

"Oooh, we got you. You said he's good looking," Amy says in a squeaky tone.

"Right. I've finished eating, and it's time to get ready and get in the van with dad for today's work." I hope mentioning that I have work to do gets them off my back.

"I'm not done with this subject," my sister teases and smirks at me.

"I believe you," I tell her, and she walks away. Heading upstairs.

"You take care and have a good day with your dad," my mum says.

"I will. See you later."

I head to my room and get changed into my work uniform.

ON THE PITCH

Damn. I hadn't thought of what others would think about the timing of me and Kyle coming out at the same time.

If my mum and Amy realise it, I wonder who else.

I can deal with the light banter and jokes about it from my family, but what if other people take it too far?

Shit. Now I am worried about what the lads on the team may think of this.

As far as I am aware, they don't know about me or Kyle, and I'd like it to stay that way, at least until me and him are ready for the others on the team to find out. I think some of them will be okay with it. But others I'm not sure about.

I can deal with any backlash, but Kyle. Him I'm not sure about and I have to protect him from any trouble someone may stir up. I would hate myself if anyone was causing Kyle trouble, and it was my fault why.

I cannot let that happen.

He's my best friend and I will defend him until the day I draw my last breath. And I know he would do the same for me.

Chapter 12
Mark

"Hey, Mark. Glad you came," Kyle's dad greets me at the door. Looking like his usual cheerful self. Patting me on the back.

"Hey Ben. Happy to be here and thanks for having me round for dinner."

"No problem. You know me and Sam like to host. Anyway, come on in." He nods his head, signalling for me to step inside his house. "Kyle and Sam are in the kitchen."

Ben leads the way through the cosy, spacious living room to the kitchen.

"I am so happy you're here, Mark," Sam welcomes. She pulls me in for a hug and a quick peck on my cheek.

"Oh, look at you two," she stands in the centre of the kitchen, looking at me and Kyle. "You are both fully grown, handsome men now. Where did the time go? I remember when you both were barely up to my neck and now tower above me." She often gets all sweet and nostalgic about the time me and Kyle were teenagers. I too have reflected on how quickly the years have gone by since finishing secondary school. Our last day there seemed like it was only a few months ago. Yet, me and Kyle are both now in our early twenties.

"Are you boys ready for the match?" Ben asks us.

ON THE PITCH

"I am, but I don't know about slow poke here," I joke.

"Who are you calling slow poke? I'm faster than you," Kyle retorts.

"Erm, well, you not stopping my goal from me the other day would make you the slow poke."

"I was at the goal. I just couldn't stretch my arm out any further to stop it."

"You wouldn't have needed to stretch your arm out if you had got to your goal just a couple of seconds earlier." I smirk hard at him. We both enjoy it when we have heated talks about our games with each other. It's an element in our friendship that has brought us closer over the years.

"We can settle this again next time." Kyle stands proud.

"Next time will be no different."

"Oh, we will just have to see about that, mate."

"Kyle, you know the definition of insanity is doing the same thing again and again, expecting different results each time," I clap back.

"Ooooh, he's got you there, son," Ben comments.

"Dad!" Kyle barks out.

"And just like with football, Mark has defeated you in the art of debate," Sam adds.

"Now I know why you wanted Mark here. So you can all tag team me. Wait till Sarah shows up. She will have my back."

"I always have your back, Kyle. Unless it comes to shitting on you with your parents. You know I can't resist that."

He knows I will always have his back, no matter what.

I cherish these moments with his family. The way his mum and dad have made me feel welcome every time is wonderful. The way they are with me is the same as my parents are with Kyle.

It's wonderful that out of our friendship, our own parents became friends too, and each family loves the other. Making us feel like one big, loving family.

It's great and I do not take it for granted. I hope I will always have beautiful connections like this, lasting throughout my life.

Ding dong!

"That will be Sarah. I'll go get her," Kyle tells us and walks to the front door.

"When did you get a doorbell?" I ask because I did not see it when I knocked.

"We've had it for ages," Ben tells me.

"He never pays attention to what's around him, dad," Kyle calls out as he continues walking to the front door.

I hear Sarah's voice and him greeting her. It's been a while since I last saw her. I know she plays an important part in Kyle's life, just as much as I do. I'm glad he has another close friend. It's nice knowing that he has many people in his life he can count on for support, and I am honoured to be one of those people.

"Hi Sarah," I welcome her.

"Mark. I'm glad to see you. It's been a while." She comes in for a hug and welcomes Ben and Sam.

After some time, me, Kyle, and Ben sit in the back garden. Soaking in the hot sun and feeling the cool breeze.

"Did you watch the derby match the other day, Mark? Me and Kyle did." His dad asks me.

"I missed the first half but caught the second. It didn't look like we were doing good from what I've been told about the first half, but I thought Everton played a good game." I give him my response.

ON THE PITCH

"Are you giving them a compliment? Some Liverpool supporter you are," Kyle teases.

Before I can say anything, Sarah joins us. Sitting beside Kyle and under the parasol.

"Oh, you boys talking about football again?" She mocks.

"Of course we are. You should know that by now. It's all we talk about," Kyle tells her.

"If you two were straight, I'd guess you would be like most men. Talking about footy and women all the time," Sarah jokingly says.

I'm fine with her knowing about me. I mentioned to Kyle that he can tell her about me being gay too.

"Nope. When it's just me and Kyle, we now talk about sexy muscular men and dicks."

"We sure love talking about dick," Kyle adds.

We both laugh across the space between us and realise both Ben and Sarah now look uncomfortable.

"Well, I'll leave you boys to talk about that amongst yourselves. Care to join me, Sarah? Or do you also want to partake in this elegant conversation about the male appendage?" Ben says with his witty, humorous tone.

"I think I'll join you," she answers.

Just as they both get up, Sam stands by the patio door and shouts, "Dinner's ready. Ben, can you give me a hand, dear?"

"Coming, darling," he gently calls out from the table area.

"So, Mark. How have you been?" Sarah kindly asks me.

"I've been swell Sarah. Thanks for asking. How have you been? Kyle told me you got promoted at work recently. Congrats."

"Thanks Mark. Yeah, my new job has been great, though a little stressful. Being on call at the surgery can be annoying, but the pay bump I got more than made up for it."

"Ooh nice. Maybe you can take us all out on a summer holiday," Kyle says.

"Mmm, not anytime soon. For now, I am focusing on building back my savings. Getting my house, made a big dent in my bank account."

"That's a good idea," I tell her.

"Hey, why don't the two of you go on a summer holiday together? Go to one of those nice gay resorts. I'm sure you will both love the view and I'm not just talking about the sun." Sarah smiles gleefully at her suggestion.

"I don't know. I'm not sure if I can bear to watch Mark here, flirt awkwardly," says Kyle.

"Hey, my flirting game worked on Beth. I see no reason it won't work on some hunks on the beach," I say in defence.

"Mmm, hunks on the beach," Kyle says with a dreamy soft voice.

"Gosh. You two were already close with each other, but I think your shared interest in men is going to make you even closer. Heck, you may get competitive on who pulls the most men," Sarah adds, and her words are adding a bit of excitement to me. The more we discuss this gay holiday resort idea, the more I actually want to do it.

"I wonder what would happen if we both fancied the same men. I think I would come out on top," I declare.

"Are you hinting that you are a top," says Kyle. The edge of his lips curl into a teasing smirk.

"Nope. I'm simply stating that I can pull more men than you, if we were to go on holiday together."

"You keep telling yourself that. Besides, with my ass, I think I can easily get the attention of other gay men. All I would have to do is wear something tight and they would be all over me."

"Are you hinting that you're a bottom?" I teasingly question him.

"Nope. I simply state that I can pull any man I want with this eye magnet." He slaps his ass after raising it off his seat.

"Gosh, you two are already flirting with one another. You both don't need to go abroad. You may as well fuck each other," Sarah jokes. At least I think she's joking.

Her comment either way stuns both me and Kyle. I see Kyle looking stiff, clearly not sure what to say or do.

Sarah catches on and quickly looks back and forth between the both of us.

"Guys, I was joking. Jeez," she says.

"I know that. I was just... urm, shocked is all. Just was not expecting you to say anything like that," Kyle say to her.

"Yeah, me too," I tell her.

She looks settled now. I don't think she thought her comment would have the effect it did on the both of us. I know why I was stunned by her words.

Because her words are true to me. I want Kyle more than as we are right now. Sure, I know how sexy he looks, and he would probably be very good in bed. But what I desire most is to be closer to him and for him to be closer to me.

Opening up to each other more than we already have. I dream of our hands clasping with each other. Our chests beating together in a tangled embrace. Holding him and letting him know he will forever be safe with me. And that where he goes, I go.

"All this talk of sexy hunky men has got me horny now," Kyle tells us.

"Great, cause we really needed to know that," Sarah replies. "If you're so horny, just rub one out later."

"I may just do that. Thanks for the idea, bestie," he smiles at her. Squinting his eyes as he does so.

"With your right hand?" I guess.

"What?" He looks puzzled.

"Your right hand. Remember? I guessed that was the hand you wank with. So, is it?"

"That's my queue to leave." Sarah gets up, but just as she does, Sam shows up.

"Come on in. Dinner is served", she tells us and the three of us walk back inside the house.

I can smell the BBQ chicken wings as I step past the patio door.

"Smells good. Your cooking is great as always," I compliment her.

"Thanks, Mark," Ben says. Taking the credit.

"Oh please. You cooked for like the last few minutes. I did most of it." Sam lightly shoulder bumps him. Their relationship is something to admire. They have been together for over twenty years, and they haven't lost the spark they had from when I first met them. I hope I am lucky enough to have a marriage as good as theirs.

With the dinner table and food set, Ben walks in with our drinks.

"Let's feast," he vocalises, and all five of us enjoy the meal.

For the next half an hour, we eat, drink and talk. Enjoying each other's company and catching up with one another. It's a wonderful moment and I hope we can have more experiences like this more often.

Someday, Kyle and I will move out of our homes, and we probably won't have enough time to create memories like this with our families. So best to make the most of it while we can.

"Well, that was wonderful. Thanks Sam and Ben. I enjoyed that," I thank the both of them.

"Thanks sweetie," Sam says. "You're always welcome. You too, Sarah."

"I know and thanks," Sarah replies. Donning a bright smile.

An hour later, and it's just me and Kyle at his place. Ben and Sam have gone out and gave Sarah a lift back to her place.

"Your parents sure know how to make an enjoyable meal," I tell him as we settle on the living room couch.

"They sure do. Anyway, thanks for coming."

"No problem. You know I enjoy coming over here to see you all," I say.

"I know that. Same goes for me and your place."

He eases further back onto the couch and succumbs to the cushioning of the pillows behind him.

"So, what did you think of Sarah's idea of going on a gay themed holiday together?" He asks me. Tilting his gaze towards my direction and slouching further down on the pillows.

"Well, it sounds good. I certainly could use a pleasant summer holiday. Soaking up the sun with clear blue skies and, as mentioned before, hunks on the beach, too. It all sounds fucking great."

"We could be those hunks on the beach for other men. We've got in good shape thanks to footy and all the time we've spent at the gym. I think we could attract some eyes." He sounds so confident.

"You've got a point. Maybe I could bag myself a twink," I tell him.

"A twink? So you like skinny and smooth, do you?"

"Not just twinks. I love a muscular, toned, athletic man. Seeing a shirtless muscle man really gets me going."

"Fuck, now I really want to do this. What you just said, has now got me excited by this idea even more," he reveals.

He leans off the couch and now rests his elbows on his knees. A more serious look taking over his face.

"Mark. You seemed really shocked earlier on when Sarah made that comment about us flirting and how we may as well fuck each other."

I see where this could go, and I am not ready to have this conversation.

"Yeah, of course I was. I just wasn't expecting her to say that." I hope that satisfies him and he changes the subject.

"Same here, but it's just. I don't know."

Good Kyle. Not knowing is good, and I hope it stays that way for now.

He leans further to me, and I think he senses my uneasiness about this movement as he pauses.

We're now much closer than before, and I think the conversation is only going to get heavier.

"Mark, I-."

Please stop Kyle. Is what I want to say, but that would upset him, and I never want to be the reason he becomes upset.

"Want to talk to you about something."

ON THE PITCH

"What about Kyle?"

I can feel goosebumps on my arms and my heartbeat pounding heavier. The sense of nervousness washes over me.

"Well... it's just since both of us came out, I have felt more comfortable about telling you something."

With a turn of my head, I look away from him and take in a deep breath, hoping it helps me compose myself.

I turn back round to face him, and his dreamy ocean blue eyes catch the attention of mine

"Mark, I-."

Instinctively, I dive my head towards him and plant a kiss on his lips.

The feeling of him on my lips sends a surge of adrenaline through me.

I have thought about this so often and it is finally happening.

Kyle bites my bottom lip and tugs his arms around me, with his right arm around my waist and his left over my shoulder.

Slowly, he pulls me closer to him and I embrace him in my grasp to.

Our lips continue to explore each other's. The saliva forming between us produces a small sound, which is now the only thing to hear in the room.

With both of us picking up the pace with our lips, I softly caress his neck, while he reaches further up my back with his hands.

"Mark," he softly whispers my name and pulls me down with him over to his side of the couch.

Hearing him call my name pulls me out of this trance and I realise I have taken this too far.

"I... I'm sorry Kyle. Oh, shit. I'm so sorry." My voice croaks as I spoke too quickly.

I hastily lean off him and shift further away from him.

"Mark," he calls me again, with a look of shock but also sadness in his eyes. Sadness that I have now caused.

"Shit. I'm sorry. I'm so fucking sorry, Kyle. Fuck, I've ruined everything."

Tears dwell in my eyes and fall down to my cheeks.

I pick up my bag and head for the door, as I want to escape this awful situation I have caused.

"Mark, please don't go," he pleads. A tone of desperation in his voice, crying out for me.

"I'm sorry, Kyle." I say to him one more time, finding the strength to look back at him as I speak.

My voice is now deep and stifled from my tears as I feel myself about to cry even more.

I close the door behind me and walk to my car.

Quickly, I get in and turn the ignition on.

"Fuck!" I curse out to myself.

I've fucked things up big time.

I may have just damaged the relationship with my best friend... forever, and it's all my fault.

Chapter 13
Kyle

"Shit," I softly murmur to myself. I tussle over my pillow and stare at the ceiling. I've only just woken up and what happened yesterday with Mark is already on my mind. Seeing his crying face and hearing his broken voice wrecked me. I could barely get to sleep last night.

I wish I had said more to him. I wish I had let him know I wasn't upset, but then that would be lying. I only became upset when he walked away and saw him cry.

"Fuck!" I curse out to myself again.

He didn't have to walk away. We could have talked about happened between us.

We could have talked about our first kiss.

I still can't believe I can say that now. That my best friend kissed me, and I got to kiss him back. I have been dreaming about this for so long.

For a long time, I always thought our first kiss would be filled with passion and a rush of euphoria.

Our kiss had passion, but that quickly evaporated when Mark freaked out and backed off.

Dammit.

I just wish he gave me the chance to let him know I am afraid too. Afraid of where this could take our friendship, but that we can figure this out together.

We always figure things out together. Have done so since we became friends. But I don't think this is something that we can easily conquer.

One clear look at him yesterday was enough to tell me that.

I feel a tear stream down my cheek and my throat swell up as I continue to picture his tearful face. It hurts. It truly fucking hurts to see my best friend like that and even more so, that I was the reason.

How can I go about my day, knowing my best friend is out there and in pain? That the last time we spoke, he walked away, and I didn't muster up the strength to speak up and reassure him we can work through this. We can come out on top. Just as we have done before when we've had arguments.

I raise myself up and lean against the pillow.

I have to get up and do something. Anything to get my mind off this.

If I don't, I will just be wallowing in misery all day in my bedroom and as much as I could easily do that, I just can't. I have to pick myself up and trust that in time, things between me and Mark will work itself out and everything will go back to normal between us.

I yawn and stretch my way off the bed and slide my feet in my slippers and head towards the door.

I wipe away my tears and take in a deep breath before leaving my room.

I take a moment to compose myself. Mentally preparing to face the day as soon as I leave my room.

ON THE PITCH

You can do this, Kyle. Just act as your regular self and don't think of Mark.

I never would have thought I would have to not think of my best friend, just so that I can make it through the day, but here I am doing just that.

With hesitation shaking through me, I pull my door open and leave my room, even though there is a feeling inside of me that is telling me to go back.

To hide away and crawl back into my bed and succumb to this new sharp feeling of sorrow that I have never felt before.

I could so easily do that, but I won't.

I will take the day with one little step at a time, and right now those steps lead me downstairs and into the kitchen.

"Morning," I make myself known to my parents.

"Morning sweetie. I'll make you a coffee now," my mum kindly offers.

"Morning to you, too. Did you get much sleep last night?" My dad asks me, and a sense of worry strikes within me. Can he tell something is up with me? Because yeah, I got very little sleep last night, but I won't tell them why.

I don't want them to worry about my friendship with Mark. Everything will be fine. It always is with Mark. That's one of the things that drew me to him. He makes everything fine in my life by just being there.

"Nope. I didn't fall asleep until much later than usual last night. It happens sometimes." I keep my voice calm and stoic, hoping they will think nothing of my answer.

"We have nights like that, too. Here's your coffee." My mum sets my mug on the coaster next to me.

"Thanks, mum."

I get up to make myself a bowl of cereal, which is what I usually do every morning, and I am going to keep doing the usual stuff I do every day. Act out like this is a regular day because it is.

"What time did you two get back? I didn't hear the door open." I say and sit myself back at the table with my cereal.

"Oh, we didn't get back in till around half 11," my dad answers.

"Later than I thought you'd be," I tell them.

"Well, we met up with Rebecca and Peter while we were out and then we all went to the pub."

A sense of agitation tightens within me upon hearing my mum mention Mark's parents. Anything to do with Mark, I want to avoid for the rest of the conversation. I worry that even mentioning his parents could lean into talking about Mark himself and what we did last night.

"What time did Mark leave here last night?" My mum asks.

"Erm, about eight- ish."

"Really? He normally stays for longer than that," she says.

"Yeah, he normally does, but I think he was just tired and wanted an earlier night."

"Good thinking on his part. You boys need all the rest you can get. The big game is coming up soon. The Majestic Lions against The Blue Hearts."

My mum's words remind me of the next footy practice session. Shit, it's only in a few days and I'm not sure if me and Mark will be back to normal by then.

ON THE PITCH

I hope we will be.

Fifteen-minutes pass by and I have finished my coffee and cereal and decide to face the day.

"Alright, time to get ready and head on out," I tell them both.

"What are you up today?" My dad questions me.

"Erm... I think I'll ask Sarah if she wants to head into town. We haven't done that in a while."

I quickly think of an answer on the spot. I didn't have any ideas about what I was going to do for the day, but I knew I would not stay inside and dwell on my thoughts. Doing that would only lead me to think of Mark, and I really don't want to be doing that right now.

"That sounds nice. You two haven't had a day out like that for a while now."

My mum's right. Ever since Sarah moved into her new place recently, she has been too busy to do anything else.

I think I will head into town with her if she's available.

Kyle: Hey, are you free today? Want to go to town? I really need to talk to you.

"I've just sent her a text," I tell my parents.

I head back into my room and get changed into fresh clean clothes as quickly as possible, because the longer I spend in my room, the more I will just want to curl up on the bed, feeling sorry for myself.

I can't do that, and I know Mark wouldn't want me to do that either.

Sarah: Yeah, that sounds great. I'll see you later.

Great. Sarah is free. She is just the person I can talk to about this. Sarah has always been a shoulder I can lean on, and right now she is the only person I feel the most comfortable talking to about what happened last night.

Kyle: Great. I'll see you then.

I send her my reply and head out the front door. Taking the day with one step at a time.

Chapter 14
Mark

Dammit, how could I have been so stupid? I gave into temptation and kissed my best friend, and I have hated myself for being so careless ever since.

It has been over twenty-four hours since I kissed him, and I still can't get over myself.

I don't know what came over me.

I had no plans or intention of doing what I did, but that doesn't matter now. The kiss happened, and I have fucked up our friendship. Even if we remain friends after all this, we may never be as close as we once were, and I cannot fucking bear the thought of that.

I don't think there is a universe where we remain friends but aren't best friends. With Kyle, it's all in or all out. My heart can't just have a sliver of him. It needs all of him. As a friend or as a lover.

Though the prospect of us being something more than friends has probably diminished to zero and it's all my fault.

Had we not been alone in that moment, none of this would have happened. Things between us would still be how they usually are. We could be hanging out right now. Yet I am in my room all alone, doing college coursework for my apprenticeship. On a Saturday of all days.

We've got another practice session with the team coming up shortly, and I don't expect things to go back to normal before that happens. Which is not ideal, as we all need to be on par and in sync with one another if we want to win the big match.

Worst of all, I think the next session is the last one before our next game.

Shit.

I really should just call Kyle now and ask if he wants to talk, but I suspect he may not be ready. Heck, I'm not ready.

As bad as I feel for spontaneously kissing him, I can't help but also feel relieved. Because I finally had the nerve to kiss him. I just stupidly didn't tell him I am attracted to him before kissing. I should have waited for him to say if he finds me attractive.

But man. When our lips touched, it's as if the world stopped. It was as if our kiss sealed the rest of the world off from us to let us have this intimate moment. Only we mattered in that space of time. My focus was on him and his on mine.

Feeling him close to me like that is something I will never forget.

Having his heartbeat so close to my chest sent me in a state of awe and wonder. From that point on, I wanted more of him than I ever have before, and he was giving himself to me. Allowing me to embrace him in my arms. He felt safe and comfortable enough to be vulnerable with me like that.

When he pulled me closer to him and our lips were still connected, I thought this was it. This was the real us. The pinnacle of what our friendship has been building towards for all these years.

Yet, when he called my name, I just froze and panicked.

ON THE PITCH

I panicked I crossed the line and possibly ruined our friendship. Now that we took the next step by kissing, we can never go back to being the way we were before and have now opened ourselves to making our friendship more vulnerable. That scares me.

We have always come back to each other, whether that be disagreements, arguments, or petty squabbles, but this. This is more than those things.

I just hope he's feeling okay. I hope I am not the reason he's having a bad day.

I have always protected him and now I could be the reason he's aching, and that hurts me. It really fucking hurts.

If he was in this situation with someone else, he would come to me for support, and I could offer a shoulder to cry on. But I know just who he can still turn to for support. Sarah.

Knowing that Sarah has been just as supportive of a friend to him as I have, I decide to text her. Hopefully she is free today and can spend time with him. He needs it, and I don't want him to spend the day alone, dwelling in misery.

Mark: Hey Sarah. Can you talk to Kyle today? He needs your support, and I can't be there for him right now. I'm sure he'll tell you why. Please, if you can, carve out time for him. Spend the day with him if you can. Please. It would mean a lot to me.

I press send and hope she sees it soon and can make plans with Kyle.

With the text sent, I turn back to face my computer screen and focus on my work, as best as I can do right now.

However Kyle felt this morning when he woke up, I hope he feels much better by now. He's always been an uplifting and light-hearted person, and I don't want today to be any different for him.

I crack on with my work and try to not think of Kyle for the next couple of hours. If he's with Sarah, he'll be fine.

I can't wallow in misery either. Besides, I'm sure things will work out between us. They always do.

Chapter 15
Kyle

"Today has turned out better than it started," I tell Sarah as we walk towards a nearby coffee shop in Liverpool. "And it's all thanks to you."

"Ah, no problem. Besides, I've missed our shopping days in town. We used to do this more often, but now life gets in the way. Work, family, and other responsibilities. Life sure was simpler back in school. Heck, even when we were eight-teen, life was still simple."

Her words ring true. Sometimes I miss those days. When everything in life for me was easy and I could get by with a carefree attitude. But we all have to step up as time passes us by.

"Yeah, those were simpler days back then, but I'm glad where I am at in life right now. As much as it can be difficult," I say to her.

Walking side by side with our hands full of bags from the shopping we have done around Liverpool, we turn around the corner on the street and head for the coffee shop.

We enter the coffee shop, and Sarah leads me to a lovely cosy spot that is secluded from the other customers. The area has two small, nice-looking sofas with a square wooden table placed in the middle.

She places her bags down near one sofa and looks at me.

"Okay. I'll get our orders and pay, and I ain't taking any pushbacks. This is my treat for you. So, what are you having?"

"I'll have a large latte."

"Cool. I'm getting a large espresso and when I come back, you can tell me what's on your mind." She shows me a warm and comforting smile before she walks away.

She knows there is something serious I want to discuss with her, but I haven't told her what exactly is on my mind. I mentioned to her earlier on, that I just wanted to go shopping with her around town and enjoy her company. Just simply relax first and then we come here, and I tell her about what happened between me and Mark.

I glance over towards her direction and notice that she is now standing at the side of where the baristas are at. Waiting for our drinks to be handed over.

The smell of copious amounts of coffee passes around me. So many flavours and scents, with hot chocolate also being mixed in. I enjoy this about coffee shops. As soon as I enter any coffee shop, I feel relaxed and at ease. I think it's because I associate the smell of coffee with a cosy and comforting feeling, and pleasant memories with friends, as I do often visit coffee shops with Sarah, Mark, and any of my other friends.

With Mark being on my mind for a moment, I instinctively scroll over my messages with him and debate with myself whether to send him a message or even a gif. I hope he is fine and doing ok. I hate to think he is still upset with himself. I sure would have enjoyed this day more if he were here with us. The three of us haven't spent a day out together like this for a long time. Life can simply get too busy.

I put my phone back in my pocket. I realise it's probably best I don't contact him yet, even though I really want to.

"Here you go," Sarah says from my right and places our drinks on the table between our seats.

ON THE PITCH

"Thanks. How much do I owe you? I forgot how much a large latte is?"

"Don't be silly. The drinks are on me, just like I said before." She smiles right at me. Her cheeks puffing out. I have always found her smile to be charming. It is so wholesome to see.

"Today has been great. I am so glad we came into town. Seems like it's been ages since we last came here," Sarah says right before taking her first sip.

"I know. It really has been a long time. Good thing we have the nice sunny weather for today too." The weather has been rather nice and relaxing lately. With the heat getting hotter these past few weeks, I can tell that summer is just on the cusp.

A moment of silence passes by, and I know she will want to discuss what is plaguing me. Before I tell her, I down my first sip of my latte. I let the taste soak my tongue before swallowing and then take a deep but quiet breath, all the while hoping the conversation won't become too uncomfortable for me.

"Kyle," she eloquently calls my name. "We don't have to talk about whatever is going on if you don't want to."

"Thanks, but I really need to get something off my chest and you're the ideal person to talk about it with."

"Okay then. Whenever you're ready. There's no rush."

She leans back further to the cushions on the seat, with her drink in hand.

Her brown eyes glance over at me and then back down to her mug as she takes another sip.

"Mark and I kissed."

"What!" she spits out her drink immediately, right over the table. Some of it also lands on my chin.

"Thanks for that," I say and cheekily smile at her.

I wipe away the coffee on my chin with a tissue and she wipes the table, all while looking dazed.

"You and Mark kissed? When did this happen?"

"After you and my parents left the house, when we all had dinner together."

"How did this happen and who kissed who first?"

I can tell she is really into this subject, already. Her look of bewilderment is gone and now a look of interest has taken over.

"He kissed me first. We were talking on the couch, and I spoke about my feelings, vaguely. I didn't directly tell him I am attracted to him, but I was working my way to it. I was nervous. Very nervous and he could tell I was, and the more I look back on that moment between us, I think he knew what I was going to tell him. That's probably why he felt bold enough to make the first move."

I pause for a moment to let Sarah take in everything I have just told her, and also to catch my breath.

She downs another sip of coffee. This one is much longer than the last. The heat from the mug warms her lips and her hands.

"Umph, I needed that," she says to me.

I quickly take another sip of my latte and realise something as I do.

"Shit," I abruptly say, which causes her to look at me in shock. "The more I reflect on this, the more Mark's sudden change during our kiss makes sense. He was too nervous and ridden with guilt over the fact that he took the initiative, without me confirming to him that I do fancy him. He was worried that he may have ruined our friendship. Fuck."

I take in another deep breath. My own words are painting a clearer picture in my head now, about the last moment I had with Mark.

"I probably should have realised this much sooner, but I allowed myself to become too stressed out and upset. Mostly with myself. I should have spoken up and told him right there and then that he ruined nothing, and that everything between us will be fine. I'm the one who has fucked things up between me and him."

"No. You haven't fucked things up, and neither has he. You simply had a moment of poor communication," Sarah tries to reassure me.

"Sarah, thanks for trying to help, but I'm not sure I follow."

"Look. You and Mark have been the best of friends since you met in secondary school, and that's how your relationship with him has been like ever since, as best friends. So, of course, when you both feel differently for each other, it is going to cause a change in how you communicate with one another and the dynamics between you both. You can't expect to transition easily from friends to... lovers."

She stretches those last couple of words out with a cutesy tone. Revelling in this relationship drama a little more than I thought she would have.

She loves talking about this kind of stuff, be it with people we know or celebrities.

"Y... you make a good point. No. Scratch that. You make a really fucking good point. I'm impressed." I give her a playful smirk and raise my brow.

"Why, thanks. I do my best," she gleefully says.

"But I still can't shake the feeling that what we had before maybe gone now. That solid friendship may never be the same."

"Kyle, I get that you're worried, but this is you and Mark were talking about. You'll both bounce back from this. I'm sure of it."

I know she's trying to comfort me, and I appreciate it, but the thought of not having that close bond with Mark ever again worries me to no end.

"It's just that if we open ourselves to something more than friendship, it could ruin what we have had for the longest time. I feel like if we remain as we are, we're keeping things safe. That we are not risking our friendship and rocking the boat. We are cruising at a nice pace. A pace that is familiar to us."

She eyes me after another long sip and settles her mug down next to mine on the table.

"Kyle. No one got anywhere in life without taking risks or rocking the boat. Yeah, sure, it's nice to sail at a pace that you're both comfortable with, but life can't always stay the same. You know that. The both of you do. You both came out and were your true selves. That right there is proof that you two can adapt to change and sail at a different pace."

She takes a deep breath before carrying on and I am here for her words of wisdom.

"Think back to all your one-to-one conversations and moments with Mark. It's in those moments where you two have always opened up to each other and worn your hearts on your sleeves, for no one else to see but each other. Before you two came out, you both got shtick about how close you are. People teased you two for it, but you had each other's backs. So it never phased you much. You two have always had each other's backs and I know you still will, no matter what happens."

We let the silence take hold for a moment. She catches her breath, whilst I take in what she said and really think about her words.

I see her take her last sip and she gently rests the mug on the table.

"I stand corrected, Sarah. You're really fucking good. I don't know how you are so sure about Mark in all of this, though? I am closer to him than you and yet I couldn't think of what you just said."

"It's because you're so much closer to him. that you can't see it. You're too emotionally involved, of course. You're worried about your relationship with him, so it makes sense. If the roles were reversed between us, I'm sure you'd be saying something similar to me. Also, there is another reason I am confident about Mark's role in all of this."

My eyes zone in on her and I feel my ears pick up upon hearing her.

"What's the other reason?" I ask her and wait in suspense for her answer.

"Because Mark texted me earlier today, and he asked me to spend time with you and cheer you up."

I lean slightly back and look down at the table, and a deep gasp of air escapes me. I can feel my face remain still after hearing her.

"He wanted to make sure you weren't alone today, so soon after that moment between the two of you. He woke up today upset, just like you, and he was worried about you being alone. His care for you as a friend is still there. It hasn't changed, and it isn't going to. No matter what is going to happen between you both, your care for each other will remain. That is for certain."

My heart feels heavier suddenly and goosebumps tingle over my skin.

"Can I read the text he sent you?" I ask of her.

"Sure."

Sarah hands me her phone, and I read the text she received from Mark.

Reading his message warms my heart and I nearly feel myself choke as an immense feeling of relief and happiness takes over me after I finish reading the text message.

Mark made sure that I spent the day with Sarah, knowing full well that she was the ideal person in my life to speak with about us.

"Thanks for showing me this," I say and give back her phone.

"Do you feel better now that you've read his message and talked to me about all of this?"

"Yeah, I do, but there is something else on my mind now."

"And what would that be?"

"Well, Mark made sure I wasn't alone today, but he is probably alone right now. He knew that out of the both of us, it would likely be me to talk with you, so I don't think he has anyone in his life he can connect with personally about this. He for sure won't feel comfortable talking to Simon, Jake, Tony, or anyone else on the team. Mainly because they don't know we're gay. Shit, now I feel like crap. Whilst I have had a pleasant day with you, he has most likely been in his room all day, feeling sorry for himself.

"You can change that, Kyle. Mark doesn't have to be alone for the rest of the day."

I gaze up at her with a concentrated look, sensing that she is about to say something else.

ON THE PITCH

"Meet up with him later today when we get back home. In fact, text him right now and ask if you can see him later. He may not be for it, so you don't want to show up announced."

She picks my phone off the table and holds it above the wooden surface by a few inches.

"Nothing bad will come of it, Kyle. He will either say yes or no. That is all."

I pick my phone from her hand and turn the screen on and tap on my text inbox with Mark.

"I'm not sure what to say," I tell her.

"Tell him you've enjoyed our day out together and thanks for thinking of me, and that you also hope he has been alright. Then ask him if you can visit him later and talk."

I nod my head in approval after hearing her suggestion. "Thanks Sarah."

I tap on my phone to type out my text message. My fingers shake with nerves as I do so.

I read the message back to myself, ensuring that I have written everything I want to convey to him.

Kyle: Hey, Mark.

Thanks for thinking of me. Sarah told me about you asking her to spend the day with me so that I wasn't alone. Cheers for that buddy. I appreciate it. I have enjoyed my day with her. We both have bought new clothes from hitting the high street in town as usual.

As much as a good day I have had, you have still been on mind, and I worry that you have been stuck in your room all day. I would like to come round to yours when I get back home. Can we talk then? It's ok if you don't want to right now.

Take care.

I press send and wait for him to reply.

"Done," I simply say to Sarah.

"Good. That wasn't so hard."

"Easy for you to say. I'm a nervous wreck right now, while I wait for him to reply to me."

I take my last sip off my latte and down it. Hoping it will calm my nerves, even just a little.

"Eew, I think I left it for too long. It's gone warm now," I tell her after swallowing the last ounce of my drink.

Before either of us can say anything else, I notice a text notification pop on my phone. It's from Mark.

"Shit. He's replied already," I quietly announce.

"Ooh. Well, read it then. Don't keep me in suspense any longer."

"I am now. Don't rush me," I jokingly say to her and pull the text up and read it.

Mark: Hey, Kyle.

I am glad to hear that you enjoyed your day with Sarah. Hearing that from you has made me feel better. You being okay and not alone today was my priority. I hated the idea of you being upset and in your room all day. Though I will admit, I have done exactly that. I have gone over that moment between us in my head many times and just wish I hadn't jumped the gun and kissed you right away. But hey, we can talk about this later if you still want to. I would like to speak with you in person. I think the time spent apart since then, has reaffirmed that we will always remain friends. No matter what changes between us.

I hope to see you soon.

ON THE PITCH

After reading his message, I feel myself cool down from within, and feel at ease that he wants to meet up later and talk. Though my heart sank when he confirmed he has been upset and stuffed in his room all day.

"He wants to meet me later and talk," I reveal to Sarah.

"Great. That's wonderful." Her eyes widen and her lips form into a smile.

"I feel lighter now, knowing that we're going to talk to each other."

"See? Things are getting better already, and you haven't spoken with him in person yet. I knew things would work out between the two of you. They always do."

With my lips closed, I softly smile back at her in response to her last few words. Mark was right in knowing that I would feel much better after talking with Sarah. He knows me so well.

"Well, should we get going, then?" She asks.

"Yeah, let's. We're all done here."

Sarah and I leave the coffee shop and make our way to the Liverpool Lime Street train station. Even though we both drive, we always opt for the train when shopping in Liverpool. The traffic around here is too much for us.

"Today has been great, Sarah. I miss these days between us. It feels like old times."

"Ha, and you sound old from just saying that," she teases. "But yeah, today has been wonderful. I'm glad we did this." She smiles back at me.

"Yeah, me too."

We arrive at the train station and hop on the train back to Huyton, where we both live."

About twenty minutes later, we get off the train and walk together back to our neighboured area.

"Now you chill for some time before you meet Mark later. Try to calm yourself before you see him," she advises.

"I will."

"Good. Message me if you want afterwards. If you want to, of course."

"Okay," I simply say.

We go in for a hug before we walk to our separate homes.

"Bye Sarah," I wave to her.

"Bye, Kyle," she waves back as she struts further away from me.

With a renewed sense of confidence in me, I head back inside my house. Ready to speak with Mark later.

Chapter 16
Mark

Okay, you can do this Mark. You're just going to talk with Kyle. Nothing more.

I have kept repeating that in my head since I left my house and began walking to Kyle's place.

I stand firmly at the doorstep to his house and inhale a deep breath with the intention that this will calm my nerves.

I exhale steadily and press the doorbell.

A few seconds pass, yet it feels longer than that. I kind of wish this talk with Kyle was already over with and we could get back to being how we were.

I am glad to be out of my house. Being cooped up inside my room all day was making me feel even worse.

Quickly, the front door opens, and I see his charming, shy smile.

"Hey," I mutter.

"Hey," he repeats. His tone is just as soft and sheepish as mine. "Come on in."

I step inside his house, and he shuts the door behind me.

The memories of the last time I was here flash before me in my head.

The crying, the sadness, and the realisation that I may have fucked up my friendship. But now I am back here feeling much different. I know that our friendship will last, no matter what.

He paces a few steps in front of me and I immediately feel like I have to say something. Anything to break the ice between us.

"Kyle," is all that comes out of me. He stops and turns to me. "Thanks for wanting to meet with me."

He steadily paces himself towards me, all while holding onto my gaze with his.

"I'm glad you came Mark."

He wraps his arms around my back. Hugging me close to him.

"I'm glad to," I whisper near him.

He pulls away and leads me to the living room.

The hug from him has melted away any remaining nerves I had. In its place, is now a sense of warmth and uplifted spirits.

"Oh, shit. I didn't even realise this but, is talking here on the couch too uncomfortable for you? Since, you know. This is where everything between us went tits up."

His concern for me pulls on my heart strings for a moment, but I continue to feel uplifted, knowing that he is considering my feelings.

"Yeah, it's fine. Thanks for the concern, though."

A soft smile forms on his face as he sits down.

"It's no problem. It's what best friends do. Look out for each other," he states.

"They sure do," I reply and sit down next to him. This conversation with him is already off to a great start.

The both of us are now sitting in the same spot as we were when we kissed.

"I think this is going to go much easier than expected," he tells me.

"Yeah. I think so too, but it doesn't make it less awkward."

"Ha, I know right. I'm glad to hear that you think this is awkward too. I have been so nervous waiting for you to come round."

"Well, I was just as a nervous wreck walking here. Which I am glad we met here at yours. I have been up in my room all day, so the change of scenery was very much needed."

He looks down away from me briefly and I can tell he must be upset by me mentioning I was alone.

"Mark, I'm sorry to hear you have been alone all day while I was having fun with Sarah."

"Kyle. There is no need to apologise to me. You know I asked Sarah to spend the day with you. You were my priority in all of this."

"I know that, but I just can't help feeling guilty that you were alone and upset."

"Well, I wasn't completely alone. I had Amy and my mum and dad with me throughout the day."

"Yeah, I know that, but I mean, you were alone by not speaking to anyone about us. With Sarah, I could talk to her about my worries. She was there for me as a form of emotional support. You didn't have anyone you felt comfortable talking to about this."

He looks sad again, but I find it cute. Even when I am trying my best to tell him that my day wasn't too bad, he still feels sad about me. It's nice to know I have a friend who looks out for me the way he does.

"What's with the huge grin?" He asks me, as he smiles himself.

"I'm smiling because we're already back to our usual selves with each other and it didn't take long for that to happen," I say.

The realisation seems to have hit him, and he leans his head back as a sign of acknowledgement.

"Oh... yeah. You're right. Wow! That really didn't take that long. I thought the conversation would have taken much longer for us to get things back on track."

"Same, but I suppose this is a testament to what good friends we are to each other."

"Ok, now you're getting cheesy," he says, followed up with a laugh.

"Yeah, I suppose I am," I say and chuckle to myself.

A moment passes by, and we're just giggling and looking at each other.

This moment right now is much different from the last time we sat on this couch in his parent's living room.

His warm smile melts my heart. Seeing it has always brought out a glimmer of happiness in me. Only his smile does that to me. Only he does that for me. He always has and always will.

"So, urm... I think we should address the elephant in the room." His words make my stomach drop. I knew we had to discuss it, but I just wished this conversation had already happened.

"Yeah, we do."

He looks directly into my eyes, and for a few seconds, he says nothing. The silence is only adding to my desire for this to be over with quickly, but I know we both have to go at our own pace, at which we feel the most comfortable.

"Well, I'm just going to come out and say it. Mark. I am attracted to you, and I assume you're attracted to me."

Another moment of silence passes us by, but this time it's due to me.

It's great to hear him say that. It makes me feel much better when I reflect on him kissing me back. I feel more at ease now.

"Yes, I am attracted to you. I have been for a long time," I reveal to him.

"I suppose the mutual attraction makes this easier than, doesn't it?"

"It does." I let out a light chuckle and smile again.

"Mark, I have been thinking why you pulled away from me when we kissed and why you were upset, and I think it might be the same concerns I have been having."

He draws out a long breath before revealing his concerns. "Is it because you were worried about what would happen to us as friends if we were to go forward as something more?"

His words hit me hard and yet, also provide another layer of assurance, now that I know he has the same concerns as me.

"Yes, that's exactly why I broke off the kiss. It scared me when I had thought I took things too far and ruined our friendship. I couldn't bear the thought of that. The possibility of us not being friends anymore or simply not as close was awful to think of, and I thought it was all my fault. I didn't want to ruin something I hold dear to me. I cherish our friendship so much, Kyle."

A The look of joy on his face begins to grow, now that he understands just how important our friendship means to me.

"We always come out on top, no matter what." He closes his lips and smiles at me, with his cheeks puffing out.

"We always do, and now I know that will never change," I simply say.

"I'm glad we're back to our usual selves."

"Me too," I add.

"Hug?" He opens his arms out, ready for me.

"Of course."

I lean over to him with my arms open for him and we both embrace each other for a moment. We both pat the other on the back as we pull away.

"So, now with that over. I just have to say this. You are a great kisser," he tells me.

"Why thank you. You're not so bad either. I really didn't want to pull away. Those lips of yours felt so good," I tell him, and it feels so good that we can already talk about the kiss in a positive light. The light-hearted conversation is something I very much needed after spending most of the day in my room, alone.

"Seriously though, the way your lips moved on mine was amazing. My god, and your tongue skills are amazing," he proclaims.

"O...k. I think you're getting really into this now," I jokingly say.

"Hey, you're the one who kissed first. All that kissing with Beth really paid off."

"If you're trying to flirt with me to get me to kiss you again, mentioning my ex-girlfriend is the quickest way to lose my interest."

"Good point," he states.

"Do you want to kiss again?" I ask, but already regretting it and wish I could undo what I just said.

"I think it's best to leave that for a later point. For now, let's just enjoy us being friends."

"Hmm, am I being friend zoned?" I jokingly say, and he lets out a soft cackle. "You're right though. I think it's wise to just stay as we are for now and will come back to this when it feels natural for the both of us."

"Yeah, that sounds like a good idea," he mumbles.

Our eyes lock onto to each other. My brown irises on his blue. No sound in the room. Only silence, yet it doesn't feel awkward. It feels comforting that we can be like this even as friends.

"So, are you coming to footy. practice tomorrow? It's the last practice session before the big match," I ask him and break the silence.

"Of course. I have to get in as much practice as I can. I have got no work commitments, so I can come."

"Nice. That's good to hear. Truth be told, I was dreading practice if we weren't back to us being the good friends that we are."

"Me too. It would have been horrible, and I know I wouldn't have been able to focus properly."

"Same," I tell him. "Plus, if you were to miss out on practice before the upcoming match, it would piss Jake off, just like the last time you missed a session."

"Oh, well then, maybe I should miss it."

"Please don't. I can't deal with his shitty attitude again," I joke.

He chuckles again, and it's wonderful to hear. It warms my heart that I am about to leave his house in a much better state than the last time I was here.

"Well, I'll get going now," I tell him. "Kyle. I'm happy that we had this conversation. It was very much needed."

"It sure was, and I'm happy that we spoke to each other."

We get off the couch and he leads me back to the front door.

"I'll see you tomorrow then at practice," I say.

"Yep. See you then."

He opens his arms out and we hug each other one more time and pat the other's back before pulling away.

"See you," I say and head on back home.

My chest and heart feel light as I walk further away from his house. It's as if my soul is at ease knowing that me and Kyle are back to being close friends again. With each step I take, my lips slowly grow into a smile that I can't resist but to let it happen.

Today started out awful for me, but it's ending on a better note than I thought it would.

I may not know what will come of me and Kyle in the future, but for now I have got my best friend back, and that is more than enough.

Chapter 17
Kyle

"Hey, what's up, buttercup?" I say to Mark from behind, catching him off guard.

"Oh, shit. You startled me," he says as he pulls cones out of a sack.

"Where are you placing the cones?" I ask.

"I'm going to make two rows that are lined side by side with each other. We can all practice our dribbling through them by crossing over from one row to the next. Once you get to the top, you turn around and dribble back to the starting point."

"Excellent stuff. We haven't done that for a while now."

"I've already told the others about this in the group chat. They should be here any minute now," he says.

"Is there any reason you asked me to arrive at the pitch early?"

He glances at me with a dashing smile.

"Yeah, well, I thought since were back to normal that you may want to have a one-to-one talk before the others show up, just like we usually do."

"Oh, sure. I am more than happy to continue these talks with you."

That is very much true. I jumped with glee earlier this morning when I read the text message from him, which said the usual thing that I expect from him and that is to meet him at the pitch early.

A feeling of joy spurt through me when I finished reading his message and replied to him.

"So," is all that comes out of me and there are a few seconds of me internally debating whether I want to ask him what's on his mind. "Have you thought more about going forward as something more?"

I feel foolish already as soon as I ask him, but he slowly turns his head towards me and shows that bright, soothing smile of his.

"Kyle, it was only yesterday we had that talk."

"That doesn't really answer my question, though." I teasingly smirk at him.

"Playing tough, are we? Well, fine. I have thought about what we would be like as a couple when I was lying in bed last night, trying to go to sleep," he answers.

"And what did you think of exactly?"

"I thought about how we would transition from friends to boyfriends. How our parents and friends would react to the change, and how we would be like with each other and... well, that's it, really."

The lingering pause as he trailed off does not go unnoticed by me, and I think he knows that.

"Come on. There's something else right. Please tell," I voice in a cutesy tone.

"No. There isn't anything to tell."

"That is bullshit, and you ain't fooling me. Now come on Preston. Reveal all of your inner thoughts to me," I tease.

"Back to using my last name, I see. You're going to keep calling me by that until I tell you what you want to hear, aren't you?"

"Yup. You got that right," I say with a nod of the head.

"Fine," he says, followed by a light puff of air from his mouth. "I have also thought about what the sex between us might be like."

I feel my jaw hit the floor and my eyes widen in shock. I was not expecting him to say that.

"I didn't expect you to say that," I tell him.

"Dammit. Now I wish I had just let you continue calling me by my last name."

"It's not bad. We already know that we are both attracted to each other."

"Yeah, but until this point, neither of explicitly mentioned anything about physical attraction."

Hearing him mention physical attraction causes me to have a sudden idea that I know I can tease him some more with.

"Soo, what is your favourite feature of mine, besides my eyes, because you're always staring at them. So I know you already like them."

He blushes and I see his cheeks are appearing more red.

"Awe, you're blushing," I tell him.

"No, I'm not," he says with a cheeky smile.

"Yes, you are. I can show you with the camera on my phone."

Just as I pull my phone out from my shorts pocket, he caves in.

"Ok, ok. I am blushing. I just wasn't expecting you to ask that question, is all."

"Well, go on. I'm waiting," I teasingly say.

"You're really enjoying this, aren't you?"

"I sure am. Now come on. Tell me," I beg again.

"Fine. It's your ass," he reveals. His answer straight and to the point.

"My ass. What is it about my ass you like?"

"Ugh, when will this end?" He laughs and turns his whole body to me now that he has pulled every cone out of the sack.

"If you tell me what it is about my ass you like, I'll tell you my favourite physical feature of yours. Deal?"

"I already know it's my eyes," he says.

"I do like your eyes too, but I have something different for my answer. So have we got a deal?"

"Fine," he huffs and puffs, all while looking cheerful with himself. I think we're both enjoying this moment between us.

"I like your ass because it seems nice and round, bubbly, and I imagine those ass cheeks of yours can be quite bouncy."

I am left stunned yet again and I stare at Mark, as I can't believe he imagines my ass cheeks being bouncy. That is the part I am surprised by the most. Does he imagine my cheeks sexually?

"Hellooo?" He calls out.

"Oh, sorry. I was, urm, well, I didn't expect your answer to be so... detailed," I tell him.

"It was the bouncy ass comment. That is what you're most shocked by?"

"Yes," I answer.

"Well, you wanted me to answer, and I did. Now it's your turn. What body part do you like of mine?"

I pause for a moment as I feel like this conversation between us has gone too far, but then I realise how easy going it has been. That talking about our physical attractions for each other doesn't feel odd or weird. It just feels right.

"Your arms. I fucking love them." I feel a slight tinge of worry when I used the word love in my answer. Going forward, I want the both of us to avoid using that word in any capacity around each other for now, at least.

"My arms, hey?" He taunts me and flexes his right arm. I can see the veins around his bicep become more visible.

"So, this is what you like?" He continues to tease. His eyes flutter at me and a playful smirk forms across his face.

With his right hand, he pulls his short sleeve on his left arm, exposing more of his other bicep. He lifts his left arm in the space between our heads and reveals his bulging triceps to me.

"Oh wow. I didn't think your triceps were that well-built. Good work on making those gains," I say to him.

"You can feel them if you want to."

"W-what?" I am shocked by his words.

"Go on. Have a feel of my biceps and triceps."

"Are you sure?"

"Yes, otherwise I would have put my arm back down. Now go on."

Slowly, I raise my hand towards his bicep, that is just a few inches away from my head.

Upon contact, I open my palm and stretch my fingers out over his flexing bicep. The skin over it is soft, yet I can still feel the hardness of the muscle underneath.

I can feel my heart beat quicker and my hand tremble. I can't believe this is happening. That he is allowing me to feel his steel hardened bicep out in the open.

"Don't forget my triceps, too."

He turns his arm inward towards his chest, so that his tricep is facing me.

"Well, go on," he encourages me.

I lay the rest of my palm over his muscle, and it feels just as solid and hard as his biceps.

After a few seconds of feeling his tricep, I can feel my dick twitch inside of my shorts.

Shit!

I hope he doesn't notice. I have to end this now.

"Good work, Mark. You're really smashing it at the gym."

I let go of his arm and place my hand beside myself.

"Thanks. I'm really proud of myself for the progress I've made. I know that might sound cocky to some people, but it's just the way I feel."

"And so you should feel proud. These are impressive results and you've been working very hard at the gym. I'm proud of you."

"Thanks Kyle. You've also being killing it at the gym too," he tells me.

"Thanks. Though I already know you've noticed the changes from my workout since you like my ass."

"You got me there," he says so charmingly.

"I've now felt your muscular arms, so I suppose you want to feel my ass now, too?"

What!

Why did I say that? Stupid me. I regret my choice of words immediately. It's too soon for jokes like that between us.

The look of his wide eyes and open mouth tells me my words surprised him.

"Wow. I was, urm... not expecting you to say that, Kyle."

"Ha, me neither. I guess I just got caught up in the moment."

ON THE PITCH

The both of us let out a soft and light chuckle. It helps to fill the awkward moment that I have now caused.

"I think we both got caught up in this moment. It was only two days ago when I was a crying mess who thought I ruined our friendship, and now where here making jokes and telling each other about our favourite features of each other. Let's just take things slowly, as we said we would."

"Yeah, you're right," I tell him, but I can't help feeling that will not happen. This playful flirting with him felt so natural and so easy. It felt good. It felt right, and I'm sure he knows that, too.

We can both promise to take things slow, but that is easier said than done. If another moment like this happens with him, I know we will both be joking and flirting once again. I don't think we can stop it now. We've opened the gates to this new dynamic between us and we cannot seal it off. The new 'us' is here to stay. I know it.

"Time to start practice now. Simon, Tom, and Jake have arrived with the others too," he informs me.

I turn to face the same direction Mark is and see the others walking over to us. All of them are in their football kits and with bags in their hands, ready to start our last practice session before the next game against the local rival team, the Blue Hearts.

"Hey," Mark vocalises across the space between us and them.

We both pace ourselves towards the others. As we get closer, I see Jake has a sour look on his face, though that isn't surprising. This time, something about it feels different. Jake is gazing at me and Mark.

"Alright lads. How's it going?" Tony welcomes us.

"I'm good Tony," I reply. "Are you guys ready for our next match? Those boys from Manchester seem like they just might win against us."

"What? Nonsense," Simon scoffs. "I'm sure we will be more than enough to beat them. We just need to keep practicing. So let's put some real good fucking effort into this training session."

"That's the spirit, Simon," Mark says, as he lays down the cones on the grass, for all of us to practice dribbling the ball through.

"Yeah, come on. Let's smash this," Tony triumphantly says, and fist bumps the air.

The other players on the team start practicing with the cones laid out for them. I've gotten to know the other players well, but I'm still not as close to them as I'd like to be. I think getting to know the people you're playing with in sports is very important. It helps to build camaraderie amongst the players, which I believe translates well when playing. The connections forged off the pitch help us to be in sync with one another when playing. I know that is certainly true for me and Mark. We know it and so does everyone else who has played with us or spectated us. We have been told many times how effective we are when we play close with each other. That has been something I have become proud of over the years. The improvements myself and Mark have made, and how much more skilful we have become.

"Alright. Time to start, fellas," Mark says after placing all the cones on our side of the pitch, across from the other players as they have already begun.

"Aye, aye captain," Simon jokes as he steps first in line.

It's a common belief amongst all of us that Mark would make a great captain of the team someday.

ON THE PITCH

Simon rests the ball under his boot, waiting for Mark to give him the signal. "3...2...1. Go!"

Simon shoots the ball across to the first set of cones and dashes forward to reconnect with it. He quickly fires the ball across to the other cone with the side of his boot and follows up after it. He does the same thing again once he crosses back to the side he started with. Repeatedly crossing over in a zig-zag trance, all while advancing to the end of the cones.

"Good work, Simon," Mark cheers him on. "Now do the same, coming back down and pass the ball to Jake."

Simon follows up on Mark's instructions and zigzags his way back to the starting point to pass the ball over to Jake.

"Good work," I hear Jake say to Simon and he stops the ball with the bottom of his boot, after Simon gently kicks it towards him.

"Thanks," Simon quips and jogs past the rest of us to the back of the line.

"Go on, Jake," I cheer, but he just looks at me with the same scowling facial expression he welcomed me with when he arrived earlier on.

He says nothing to me and dribbles the ball through the cones. The same way Simon did seconds ago.

A moment later, Jake returns to the starting point and passes the ball to me without so much as even looking at me.

I decide not to bother asking him what his problem is with me and instead, focus on the task at hand.

I quickly dash through both rows of cones, and I can tell that I am improving with my dribbling skills. I am quicker on my feet than I ever have been before.

"Well done, Kyle. You're improving a lot," Mark says out loud and claps his hands for me as I pass the ball to Tony.

I look back at Mark and see him cheerfully smiling at me. I smile back and give him a thumbs up as I get back in the line.

Every player on the team continues this method of practice for fifteen minutes, which is much longer than how we usually run this test, but we really have to get our A-game on and practice as hard as we can if we want to win our next game.

"Alright, that's enough of that," Mark calls out. "It's time we have a proper game now. Let's all split into an even number of two teams."

All of us gather around in the centre of the pitch, including the players that were practicing on the other side. We line up, waiting to be selected by Mark and the captain, Jason, to be on their teams.

I notice Jake in the corner of my eye, slowly pacing himself towards me.

"Ugh, I saw how you two were smiling at each other before. Please do not make it that obvious when we're facing against other teams," Jake whispers near me, with his head slightly turned towards me.

Slowly, I twist my head to face him.

"What are you talking about, Jake?"

"Look, I know you are gay, and I know Mark is, too. Before you ask how I know, my mum overheard yours and Mark's mum talking in a shop when they mentioned you two coming out."

An unsettling feeling sinks within me. I didn't want anyone else on the team to learn about this detail about me and Mark. Especially not Jake, with how he's been such a pain in the ass when I have missed practice sessions.

ON THE PITCH

"So, what's it got to do with you?" I grip my hands together in front of me, as if we're in line facing a penalty shoot.

"It's got nothing to do with me and like I said, I don't care that you two are gay, but just don't fucking make it obvious like you did before." His tone becomes more angry and thicker with each word he says.

"Jake. If you think smiling and giving a friend the thumbs up is gay, well, you've got some issues. Me and Mark are just friends. You know that and friends smile at each other and give them the thumbs up when they're proud of each other. Besides, why are you so concerned about what other teams would think of us?"

He pauses for a moment, and I can tell the players closest to us are wondering what is going with me and Jake.

"You're a smart lad, Kyle. You know how rough some fellas can be, especially when playing a match, and in the changing rooms. I don't want other players to hurl abuse at you two."

Before I can even think that Jake is coming from a place of caring for me and Mark, I know there is something else to his issue with us.

"And I don't want others to know that I am on a team with someone like you," he says to me.

That last part stings, but I am definitely not going to let him get away with that, so I decide to put him on the spot in front of everyone.

"Someone like me," I raise my voice. "What do you fucking mean, Jake, by how you wouldn't want to play on the same team as me?"

The players nearby turn their heads towards me, one of them being Simon.

Jake now looks nervous and rattled with the sudden attention.

"What's going on Kyle?" Simon asks.

"Nothing much Si. Just that Jake here doesn't want to be on the same team as me anymore."

"I didn't say that," Jake retorts and slowly backs away from me. Creating a few feet of space between us.

"What's going on here?" another player asks.

I cross my arms and stand strikingly confident at seeing Jake squirm away.

"I never said I don't want to be on the team with him. I just simply don't want other teams knowing I play alongside with someone who is gay. Think of the constant jokes they would make off," Jake finishes.

I see Simon and a few other players, including Tony, now all look at me in shock.

I continue to show my resilience towards Jake, but the sudden gaze of everyone unsettles me.

"You're gay?" Simon questions.

"Yep," I blurt out.

Suddenly, it seems everyone is aware of this conversation, including Mark and Jason, as they both stop selecting players for their teams and come forward to me and Jake.

"What's the issue here?" Jason says as he and Mark step into the crowd that me and Jake seemed to have created.

"Nothing. Everyone is making this a much bigger deal than it should be." Jake's anger is showing through his words.

"What's up Kyle?" Mark asks me.

"Oh, you know. Just Jake being a dick, as usual. He doesn't want other teams knowing he plays alongside a gay man like me."

Now my words seemed to have startled Mark. His body stiffens on the spot next to Jason and it's clear that he wasn't expecting me to have said what I have just told everyone.

"Ugh, for fuck's sake. If you had just kept your mouth shut, Kyle, none of this would have turned into a big show for everyone else to see."

"Shut up, Jake," Mark snaps back. The anger in his voice was clear for everyone to notice, even though he only said three words.

"Jake, calm down and everyone else, back away," Jason commands.

The other players slowly pace themselves to the other side of the pitch. Some of them are clearly reluctant in doing so and want to stay back for the drama.

"Jake, apologise to Kyle now. Otherwise, you will not continue to take part in today's practice," Jason says to him.

"What?" Jake cries out.

"Look lads, I'll just head off now," I tell them. "I'm not in the mood to continue practicing."

"You don't have to leave, Kyle. Jake is the one who should leave," Mark tells me. I can see a glimmer of sadness in his eyes when he turns his head away from Jake and Jason.

"I know that, but I really am just not in the mood to carry on."

I turn my glance over at Jason. "Jake can stay if you want him to continue. I know we need as many players as possible to be practicing and be prepared for the next match."

Jason nods his head to me, and I walk over to collect my bag and leave.

"Thanks for looking out for me Jason," I say to him and pass Mark. "You too. I know you've always got my back," I say to Mark and pat him on the shoulder and walk towards my bag.

With each step I take, I realise I am not as hurt about this as I thought I would have been. I think patching things up with Mark has left me in such a joyful state, that not even this mess with Jake can ruin my day. Though I am down about not continuing practice, but my heart just isn't in the spirit to play now.

I reach for my bag and lean down to pick it up, when I notice a hand reaching for Mark's bag.

"Mark. What are you doing?" I ask after I look up to see his face.

"I'm not leaving you on your own again."

"You don't have to do this for me. You should be back over there, playing with the others."

"I could do that, but it's like you just said to me a minute ago. I've always got your back and I've got it right now."

"But..."

"But nothing. Now let's head back to my place and cheer you up," he says and swings his bag over his shoulder.

"You're a good friend, Mark." I smile back at him as he rests his hand on my shoulder, and we walk back to our cars.

"I know I am," he laughs.

I am honoured that he's in my life. No matter if that's as a friend or something more. Just knowing him is something I will forever be grateful for.

Chapter 18

Mark

"Here's your coffee," I say to Kyle and rest the mug beside him on my living room table, next to the couch he's sitting on.

"Thanks." He smiles brightly at me. It's nice to see him in good spirits, even after dealing with Jake's awful attitude.

We have only just got back to my house from practice, and he's already settled in perfectly fine, as if nothing had happened.

"How are you holding up?" I ask him after grabbing my mug of tea and sit myself next to him.

"I'm good. Honestly, I really am. I thought I would be more upset about what just happened back then, but I'm not."

I believe him. He seems like his usual self, and I can normally tell when he's holding back on me. It's a skill I have learned from spending so much time with him over the years. I'm sure he can tell when I'm not wearing my heart on my sleeves.

"To be honest, I think if it had been someone else who spoke to me like that, like if it was Simon or Tony, I would be upset, but Jake has been an ass to me, anyway. So I'm not too shocked by all of this," he continues.

"Good point. I suppose you're right. Despite that, to say what he said and so overtly to with others around, well... I just was not expecting that. I was really worried for you once I saw you were involved, Kyle."

"Awe," he gushes and cheekily smiles at me. "I knew you would be."

"Ugh, you can be so full of yourself," I tease and nuzzle his shoulder back.

Our eyes remain fixed on each other's for a few seconds longer than I think we both would have liked. We quickly both look away in the same direction towards the table, trying to avoid any further temptations.

We both agreed to take things slow and figure out the new us in due time. The flirting back at the pitch was too far. Especially when I let him feel the muscles in my arms, which I really regret now, but at that moment, it felt right. It felt easy with and also really good.

"Oh, I can't believe I haven't even asked this yet, but how the fuck does he know you're gay?"

Kyle stiffens his neck straight and places his mug back down after taking a sip of coffee.

"He told me his mum overheard our mums talking in a shop about me coming out," he answers.

"Ohhh." I ponder and think about why on Earth our mums would talk about such a topic in a supermarket, but that's for another day.

"Did Jake's mum hear them mention me being gay too?"

"No. He only mentioned about me. I thought how odd it was that they only mentioned me, but maybe they mentioned you too, but his mum mustn't have heard that part of the convo."

"Yeah maybe." I nod my head after hearing his thoughts on the matter.

ON THE PITCH

"Though, I think he assumes you're gay too, because he kicked off at me when we smiled at each other, and you clapped for me after I completed my first lap of dribbling through the cones."

"Oh, how daft is he. It's now gay to be happy for your friends," I say and that gets a laugh out of him. "Anyway, enough about Jake," I say.

"I agree with that."

"Have you thought more about Sarah's fun idea of going on holiday together? Ideally at one of these gay resorts, she mentioned. I've looked online and there are some that have caught my attention."

"Have the resorts themselves caught your attention or the half-naked men featured on their websites the thing that has caught your attention?"

He playfully smirks at me and I, on instinct, smirk back at him.

"How do you know there are half-naked men on the resort websites?" I ask him.

"Well, I assume they do."

"A fair assumption, I agree, but I think you yourself have checked these resorts out. Am I right?" I nudge my head slightly towards him, still smirking as I do. Waiting for his response.

"Well, yes, I have."

"I fucking knew it," I tease.

"Hey, when Sarah described it as hunks on the beach, I couldn't resist."

"So, you have thought about this too then?" I question.

"Yes. It sounds like a good idea. Even if it doesn't turn out to be a hot sexy place with shirtless men swimming by the beach, I think us going on a holiday together in the summer sounds good. I sure could do with a pleasant break from work."

Hearing him seeming to be up for this makes me more compelled to go through with it.

"Yeah, a holiday sounds like a good idea. Though, we've never been abroad together as just the two of us. We've only ever gone with other friends. Do you think it would be weird between us?" I air my thoughts.

"Why would it be weird? It's us we're talking about." His response is so full of confidence and joy, to where I don't think he realises what I mean.

"Well, given what's happened between us lately, I just thought only us going abroad together might get awkward. Like, I know we said we would take it slow and figure things out, but us being together on holiday might complicate things."

He looks at me for a few seconds and then his gaze drifts to the side of me. His facial expression clearly signals that he's deep in thought and pondering on my words.

Casually, he leans back against the couch and slowly smiles at me.

"What?" I ask.

"I think you're overthinking about all of this and it's cute that you are," he tells me.

"How so?"

"Look, I know we're stepping into unfamiliar territory between us, but we've already kissed. So it's not like we haven't already crossed the line and besides, we're friends, so it would still be a fun holiday together. We know we will remain friends no matter what."

As usual, his words provide me a sense of comfort and bring me back down from my concerns.

"You're right. I was overthinking about it, and I know you're going to take pleasure in me saying that."

"Oh, you're absolutely right," he says with his voice full of pride, before taking another sip of coffee.

"When did you become so wise?"

"Hey, I've always been a wise beyond my years," he retorts and places the now empty mug back on the table. "Anyway, us going on holiday together would be even better now."

"How so?" I finish my cup of tea before he answers.

"Well, we're best friends who are both gay. So we can admire the hunks on the beach together and go to the gay clubs together too."

"Oh yeah," I say with wonder. "That sounds like a good time. I think we would have a lot of fun."

"We sure would." His eyes flicker as he speaks. I can tell he's just as excited about this idea as I am.

"A holiday together after the big match could either be a trip to celebrate if we win, or to have fun and forget about our loss, if you know, we lose."

"Do you think we will lose?" I ask of him.

"Honestly, I'm not sure. I know all the other lads like to talk a big game and how we'll never lose, but one team has to lose and those boys from Manchester are great. I'm sure some of their players talk the same way as some of our teammates about winning every match."

Kyle's right. The players we'll be up against from Manchester are tough and will definitely be a challenge for us.

"Win or lose, I'm just happy to be playing a big game again. It seems like it's been ages since we last played a big match. Plus, it will be fun to play alongside with you again."

He smiles warmly at me after hearing my response.

"We do make a good team. Both on and off the pitch," he says in a soft and clear tone.

"We sure do."

We spend most of the night chilling together in my bedroom, playing video games and simply talking about everyday life. Our families, our jobs and everything in between.

Just like old times.

Chapter 19
Mark

"Are you alright?" My dad calls out from the stairs after hearing the loud thud coming from me in the bathroom.

"Yeah, I'm fine. I just dropped the wrench is all when I banged my arm against the wall."

"Remember to be more aware of your surroundings on jobs like these, son. In this line of work, you'll often work in crammed spaces."

"I know that, dad," I reply softly.

"Just be extra careful, is all."

I've been working with him as an apprentice plumber for months now, but he still treats me as if I were completely new to all of this. But I suppose that's just his parental instincts kicking in. I'm sure I would be the same if I had a kid, and I was teaching them.

"How are you coming on with the pipe?" He asks as he steps near the bathroom door.

"Almost got it."

"Good pipe work, son. You've done it exactly as I would."

"Thanks dad," I barely mutter as I lay on my back and using both of my arms to tighten the wrench around the pipe.

I position the wrench back to the starting point and turn it one more time.

My biceps flex as I use my strength to tighten the wrench one last time around the pipe under the bathroom sink.

Seeing my muscles bulge and the veins become visible, I am reminded of Kyle's admiration for my arms, and I think back to the moment I let him feel them. I can feel myself smile as I reflect on that moment, and I'm sure my dad can see it.

"What are you smiling about?" His voice has a hint of a cheerful tone to it.

"Oh, just thinking of a funny moment that happened with Kyle."

My answer is genuine to some extent.

"Of course," he says, "you two always seem to make each other laugh."

"You're right," I tell him.

"It's nice that you've got such a good friend like him in your life. Good friends like Kyle don't come around often, and especially into adulthood. You're a lucky lad to have him in your life."

"I know, dad. I am very lucky indeed."

I finish tightening the sink pipe and release the wrench and pull myself off the floor.

"Good work, son. I'm proud of you. You're becoming a fine plumber."

He smiles brightly at me and pats me on the back.

"Thanks dad. I am learning from the best."

"Oh, someone's being nicer than usual. You must want something from me," he laughs.

"Not yet. I'm just buttering you up right now."

"Ha." His laugh bounces off the tiles walls. "It's not wise to tell me you're buttering up to me. Anyway, let's pack up and see to Mr Clark."

ON THE PITCH

For the next few minutes, I help clean up with dad and pack up our tools and store them back in the van.

"All done John," my dad greets Mr Clark on a first name basis. He's been a regular customer for my dad for many years now.

"Your bathroom sink is back in working condition," my dad informs him.

"Ah, good. Thanks gents. You two have done a cracking job. Here's the payment."

Mr Clark hands over the cash to my dad.

"Thank you." My dad's gracious attitude is on display.

He's always thankful, even when he receives payment for his work. He is always thankful for everything and anything.

"You're shaping up to be a fine plumber, Mark," Mr Clark says to me.

"Why thank you, sir," I reply to him.

"Ooh, and he's well-mannered, too. Where did that come from?" Mr Clark says humorously and eyes my dad.

"Oh, trust me. He's only like that with customers," my father tells him.

"Ah, because the customers are paying you." He looks back at me.

"You know it, sir," I respond.

"Ha. A smart young man you've become. I still remember the days of your dad doing a job in my home and having to go pick you from primary school when you were a little boy. Now here you are with a lean muscular build and some facial hair. The years do indeed fly by."

"They sure do," my dad says. "It seems like it was only yesterday I was doing the school runs."

He rubs his hand over my hair while reminiscing about days past.

Those days back in primary school also don't feel that far away from me either, and since then, I have met Kyle in secondary school, finished college, dated Beth, and then broke up with her, and become an apprentice to my dad. Yet these events and milestones feel like they both happened ages ago, but also not too long ago. Time can be a weird thing.

"Well, John, as much I like to reminisce about life and realise how much sooner I am to getting grey hair and wrinkles, it's time for us to leave," my father says.

"Understood, and by the way. You've already got a bit of grey hair and wrinkles."

"Cheeky," my day jokingly quips back.

"See you boys another. Bye." Mr Clark waves at us.

"Bye John."

"Bye, sir," I say.

Me and my dad get back in the van and we hear John shut his front door.

"He's very nice. I think he's become one of my favourite regulars," I say.

"Yeah, he is. He's been a loyal customer to me for a very long time. He was one of the first people who gave me a chance when I started my plumbing business."

"Really? Well, he is very loyal indeed, then."

"He sure is. I was lucky in having met him when I did."

"How come?" My curiosity has peaked from hearing him speak in a tone that hints there is more to what he was saying.

"Well, before I started my business, I was working for another company as you already know, but they weren't pulling in much business and jobs had to be shared out, given that there was an entire team of plumbers. Money was tight at the time and me and your mum were struggling to get by. So, I started my business. Thankfully, your uncle John gave me his old van for nothing, so that was one big expense taken care of. I knew some people in our area and around town had jobs that needed doing but didn't want to pay the expensive costs that many big businesses were charging. My old company being one of them. Many older people were being charged way more than they should have."

"That's terrible," I cut in.

"It is, and unfortunately, it happens a lot. So even when I started my plumbing business, me and your mum were still struggling to get by. We expected to struggle for a bit when I started this company, but not for as long as we did. That's where John comes in. He saw one of my leaflets I taped on the local news bulletin board. He called as soon as he read it and the next day I was working at his, fixing his kitchen sink, and he gave me good feedback and told as many people as he could in his life. Word of mouth goes a long way. But what really boosted things for me was that he was a member of a local group who met up every week near the local council building to discuss things happening in the community and what needs to be done. That sort of thing. Well, John told everyone about me at these meetings and even handed out copies of my leaflets that I had printed for him. Business was booming for me right after he did all of that. I never even asked him to do either."

"Wow. He really came through for you. Perfect timing from the sounds of it."

"He sure did me a solid one back then. Since then, I have always gone above and beyond for him. I always try to make time when I can for him. That's another part to learn as an apprentice, son. Be loyal to customers and treat them with respect."

"I know, and I will always keep that in mind."

"Good," he simply states.

We arrive back home.

The drive from Mr Clark's place to our house really went by fast. I guess all that profound talking with my dad really passed the time.

Before we get out of the van, I sense my dad wants to tell me something else.

"Mark. I got really lucky when I crossed paths with Mr Clark, just like how you were lucky to have crossed paths with Kyle."

I remain seated in silence after hearing him mention Kyle unexpectedly.

"Why are you talking about Kyle?"

"I simply wanted to point how a chance meeting or an encounter with someone can transform your life. You've met other people when at school or college and your friends with them still, but none of them have impacted your life like Kyle has."

"That is true," I reply to him with my voice partly broken, as I am still shocked because of the surprising turn of this conversation.

"All I am saying, Mark, is that you never know what may come out of meeting someone. Anything can happen. Be it small or big. You just never know until you see the results."

His lips form into a cheeky grin, and he opens the van door to his side and gets out.

I am left reeling in a state of disbelief.

Since when did my dad become so profound and mysterious in the art of conversation?

ON THE PITCH

He is hinting at something and if so, what?

He could just be messing with me. That would be such a dad thing for him to do.

But I don't think it is. Not this time, at least.

Chapter 20
Kyle

"Ready to hit the weights?" Mark asks, and I turn my gaze towards him as we both slow down on the treadmills.

"Yes, I think that was enough of a warmup." I let out a heavy gasp of air and walk onto the gym floor. I can feel droplets of sweat already trickle down my torso.

It filled me with a sense of joy when Mark asked me to work out with him at the gym. We haven't done that for a while now and it's great that we are still continuing things as friends. Keeping things between us as normal as they should be, but I wonder if working out with each other since our kiss will be too much. Mark has already let me feel his muscular arms once before, and he knows I like them. Like *really* like them. To the point, I want to feel his muscles wrap around me, lift me off the ground, and feel his biceps once again.

Right now, just the sight of his solid biceps snugly fitting into his short sleeve gym t-shirt drives me wild. I want to feel them, lick them and every other inch of his arms. His triceps, forearms. All of it.

"Hellooo? Are you just going to stand there?" I hear his voice.

"Oh, what?" I speak and feel myself blush.

"You were just standing still and staring in my direction for a few seconds too long," he tells me.

ON THE PITCH

"Was I? I didn't even notice. Silly me."

His lips curve into a grin. A sexy, charming grin I won't be able to stop picturing now. A grin that signals that he probably knows I was checking him out again, and that I want him more now since he laid his lips over mine.

It may have only lasted a couple of seconds, but that grin he showed as he walked past will be on mind for at least a week.

"Good. The area near the free weights is empty," he informs me as I follow him. "We've got our choice of weights to choose from," he concludes and picks up a set of 15kg weights.

"Nice. Just us two, for now at least," I say.

I grab a pair of 12kg weights and stand next to Mark, facing the mirror as we both perform bicep curls.

We stand firmly in place, raising our arms up with dumbbells in hand. Neither of us lifts our arms too fast, but go slow as it is more effective, plus we can feel the muscle burn more, which both of us enjoy.

A few minutes pass by as we continue doing biceps curls, and I feel my dick twitch beneath my shorts. Seeing Mark work his muscles out tends to have that effect on me, as well as hearing his grunts when he performs his reps. His deep, masculine groans tingle my ears and send my mind into a fantasy of us being tightly wrapped around each other. I imagine my chest against his. My neck being a target for his lips to land on, all the while our arms explore each other, and he lets out those same grunts as he kisses me.

"You're doing well there. Your form is spot on," his voice snaps me out of my fantasy.

"Oh… thanks. You're smashing it too," I try to scramble for words but also say something truthful. "I can see the difference in the size of your arms. They're definitely getting bigger."

"Well, we both know how much you like my arms," he utters, and *shit*. I sure opened myself up for that comment.

I see him smirk at me through the mirror in front of us. It's almost like he's taunting me. Teasing me with his very own reflection.

He knows I am obviously going to see him in the mirror when standing next to him, side by side. It wouldn't surprise me if he had this in mind since we set foot in the gym.

"If we were doing squats right now, I know you'd be watching me too," I counter, putting the heat on him now.

"Why, of course I would be watching. I would spot you to make sure your posture is good."

Damn, he's good. He always has a response at the ready for my comebacks.

I see his smirk melt into a gentle smile. One that melts me from the inside. A smile that brings out the butterfly feelings from within and makes me ache to kiss him again. To feel our wet lips make contact again and our tongues caught in the middle while we explore each other.

I notice him tilting his head and gazing down to my ass after he finishes a set of bicep curls.

"So I don't even need to be doing squats for you to check my ass out?" I blurt out while no one else is around us.

"No, you do not," he says as he begins another set of curls. "But I know you're checking my biceps out in the mirror." He turns to face me and shows me his sexy, cheeky grin.

ON THE PITCH

"Was it that obvious?"

"Nope, but I just wanted you to confirm my suspicions."

"Ah, you dick," I playfully speak. I can't believe he figured me out. He's good. Really fucking good.

This playful back and forth flirting with him has lit a fire within me, and I don't want it to be put out. I want it to continue. To expand till it ends with me and him in my bed, or his, or any bed. As long as we are together, and he is giving me all of him, and I give him my ass. I know he would like that very much.

"I'm done with the weights," I say to him and rest the dumbbells on the rack. "I'm going to do some squats now. You're more than welcome to come and spot me." I wink at him as I turn toward the squat rack. I purposely turn my hips slowly, allowing the view of my tightly pressed shorts on my glutes to linger on for his viewing pleasure.

"Ugh, you're such a fucking tease," I hear him from behind.

"I've learned from you."

I can hear his footsteps behind me after he puts his dumbbells back with the others.

As I reach the squat rack, I slow down and bend over, pretending to fix my shoelaces.

"Oh, come on," he cries out. "Now you're really fucking teasing me."

I quickly raise myself up, turning my head round to flash him a wink.

Within seconds, I apply the desired weight plates onto the bar with Mark's help and perform my first set.

I buckle my hips and slowly descend, with my hands holding the bar steady at 20kg.

Mark paces himself from side to side. I can see him in the mirror. He seems to be spotting me. Only focusing on my form, and not so much on my ass.

"Ugh... eh," I pant heavily after finishing my first set of ten reps.

"Good work. You've got an excellent form. It's always important to have correct form and posture for any form of exercise, but especially so when doing squats." His tone is playful but not flirty playful. Just his usual friendly tone, which I do like, but that's not what I want to hear right now.

What I want is to hear him speak with a tone that is backed up by lust, by desire, by infatuation. A tone that screams, '*I really want that ass of yours, Kyle.*'

With a deep breath taken, I start my second set, but this time, I push my glutes out further and squeeze them tight, hoping the muscles from them will be visible through the fabric of my shorts.

A few seconds pass, and I am halfway through my second set, and it's only now when Mark paces himself back and forth behind me.

I can see his gaze in the mirror, lower to my waist as I bend at the knees once more.

"Oh, yeah. Keep that up," he says. He stops walking and leans an arm against the frame of the machine.

"It took you longer enough to get looking," I say to him, in between reps.

"Well, I really did just want to make sure you have proper form."

I believe him. "Awe, thanks, but you can get back to looking now."

"Well, since you're encouraging me, I may as well."

ON THE PITCH

His cheeks puff out and he blushes, but not from embarrassment. No. I think it's from the flirty banter we've held up since entering the gym. I feel uplifted from it. Reinvigorated even, and I'm sure that's how he's feeling, too.

A moment later, and I am onto my last set after finishing another two.

I perform the first rep, but I stop, with my knees bent, when Mark comes behind me.

"What are you doing?" I ask of him.

"Helping you out. You're in a good position, but I think you can still go lower and get more out of your squats."

I'm no fool. I know what he really wants. "Is that so, or did you just come up with that excuse to have a reason to get closer to me?"

He lets out a small chuckle. "I am doing this to be closer, but I do really think you can get lower. So, let's begin."

He places his hand on both my sides, just an inch away above my waist.

Feeling his muscular hands on me sends a shiver through my back and the sides of my torso.

I do another rep and as I do so, his fingers grip more tightly around me. His touch is electric. My senses are on high alert. My chest is beating hard. An alarm is blaring within my heart, and it won't stop until he lets go.

"You good?" His calm voice cuts through the moment of silence that passed by.

"Yeah, I am. Thanks."

"Just a bit lower," he encourages, and I do as he says.

I bend my knees slightly more, and I can feel more of a burn in my glutes from reaching a lower level. The bar resting on beneath my neck becomes more strenuous on me, but nothing that I can't handle at the current weight I am squatting at.

"Good, good. Just a little more. I know you can do it."

I lower myself some more and that's when I hear, "Great! Good job. Now raise yourself back up, slowly."

I raise myself up, and rest the bar back on the frame, and catch my breath. I sense Mark stand up straight behind me, and his chest gently grazing against my back. It feels comforting to have him this close behind me. He's always said he will have my back, and seeing his reflection in the mirror, right behind me, feels right. It feels new, intimate, and calming.

It's only after looking in the mirror for a second longer that I realise his hands are still on me, but his touch has gone from a tight grasp to a light one.

"Oh, sorry. I didn't realise I was still holding onto you," his voice breaths on my neck, which sends a tingle through me.

"It's fine," I tell him.

An awkward moment of silence takes place between us. I see him slowly back away from me, giving me the space to walk away from the spot beneath the bar I had just been using.

Suddenly, he slides a workout bench across the gym floor and places it underneath the bar.

"Are you going to do bench presses?" I inquire.

"I am," he answers. "You set the bar at twenty, didn't you?"

"I did."

"Good. That's just the weight I want to try out," he says.

ON THE PITCH

He quickly adjusts the seating on the bench and does his first set of bench presses for the session.

"Mind if I spot?" I raise my brow and smirk down at him.

"Go ahead. I think it's only fair after I spotted your ass," he says before he does his first rep.

I pace the floor space around him. Going in circles, all the while, I fixed my gaze on his pecs pushing through his white tank top. I can see the sweat sliver across from underneath his arms to his waist. Oh, how I wish I could lick it off his body. To taste it on my tongue and feel his muscles at the same time.

Fuck! I can feel my cock twitch again. Now is not the time I want to get an erection, especially with other gym goers now walking past us on the ground floor.

Mark finishes his first set and takes a sip from his water bottle. "Ah," he lets out a moan of joy from being hydrated. "I needed that."

"I can tell. You're sweating," I point out to him.

"I am, and I bet you're enjoying it," he says.

"Oh, I am."

"Well, how about you get a better view and actually spot me?"

"What do you mean?" I stop in my tracks upon asking him.

"Get behind me and rest your hands over my shoulders. Make sure I don't lean the bar over more to one side, otherwise I am going to drop it."

"Understood." I nod my head to him and get behind him.

He makes out like he needs me to spot, but we both know this is just for me to get a better view of his pecs when he pushes the bar out above his chest, which will push his pecs out. That's what he wants me to see, and it's what I want to see too.

"Ugh," he groans out loud upon pushing the bar out. I'm not sure if that groan was on instinct, or on purpose for my enjoyment. Either way, I can't stop replaying it in my head.

With his first rep done, I focus and lay my hands over his shoulders. The contact with his round solid muscle is enough pleasure for me in itself. Mark has seriously bulked his arms up, and being able to feel the results is pure bliss.

With his second set underway, I focus on the sneak peek of his pecs underneath the gap from his tank top. I can see his sweat covered pecs even more when he pushes the bar out from him, which gives me an idea.

"Mark, hold the bar out for a second or two longer. Let it stay there. Don't pull it back to you so soon."

"Got it," he blurts out with struggled breath.

I'm not sure if he's figured out why I'm asking him to do this, or maybe I really did just give out solid workout advice.

He grits his teeth and pushes the bar out, and he does as I instructed. With the extra few seconds I have given, he lets the bar stay above his chest, and I swipe another look at his pecs. His round muscles are so tantalising to me. I am impressed at his hard work, but also turned on by the results.

"How are you liking the view?" His words take me out of my gaze.

"Oh, very much. So I take it you figured out why I asked you to hold the bar out for a few seconds longer?"

"Kyle, I caught on to it right away, but you ended up giving me a solid tip. Those few extra seconds really add to the muscle burn."

"Nice. Well, I'm glad to be of help."

ON THE PITCH

After finishing up another set, he rests the bar on the frame and takes a moment to rest. I see his chest heave when he inhales deeply. I notice his pecs slowly raise up and back down, all while sweat continues to trickle down.

The sight I am seeing is hotter than any gay porn video I have ever seen.

This muscular stud who is my best friend, and maybe something more, is laying on a workout bench right in front of me, giving me the best view of his sculpted work of art.

I am so glad Mark wore a tight-fitting tank top today, as it shows off his round, hardened shoulders. Shoulders that I have just touched and can still feel the tingle of excitement that ran through me when I placed my hands on them.

"Still enjoying the view, are you?" His voice cuts through the tension once other people walk past us.

"Am I enjoying seeing the muscular hunk in front of me? Nah, not really," I say in a tone that shows that I am clearly very much enjoying the view.

I look down at him and see him smiling up at me as he lies on the bench, still.

I show him a smile too before he begins his final set.

"Aren't you hard to please," Mark teases.

"Not true. I already am getting hard from this."

My smile quickly goes away, once the shock of what I had just said takes over me. A moment of panic sets in, and I worry that I may have taken this flirty back-and forth too far.

Mark looks up at me and shows me his charming smile, followed by a wink.

"I'm glad to hear I have that effect on you," is all he says, and starts pushing the weight from him.

I compose myself, and the alarm bells in me go away, now that I know Mark is completely fine with what I said. Sometimes I surprise even myself.

"Argh... ugh. Done," he says after the last rep.

He pants, and I can hear that deep masculine groan that makes me weak in the knees.

Once he gets off the bench, I can see the sweat he's left behind. *Fuck*, how I wish I could see his sweat glistening torso right now.

"You weren't kidding," he utters and glances down at my groin.

"You're bold for checking that out," I say to him.

"Hey, you're the one who mentioned your semi."

"That I did," I say and quickly glance to his waist since we're standing right in front of each other. "I see you're also rocking a hard-on," I point out.

"Hey, there is a difference. I never brought up my cock," he says in defence.

"True," I say, "but you brought up your muscles and worked them out in front of me, so you practically started this whole cock-induced conversation."

"Speaking of working out my muscles, I need to wash the sweat away." Mark huffs a gasp of air out and walks past me.

I turn to follow his direction and I can't resist peaking down at his tight shorts, hugging his ass. He's been working out his glutes more than usual. Probably trying to compete with me. Well, his ass ain't got nothing on mine.

ON THE PITCH

"Finally. Time to shower," he says upon entering the men's changing room.

Within seconds, we both take off our gym clothes and place them on the bench by our bags and cross over to the side of the room where the showers are.

We enter separate shower cubicles, so we cannot see each other, but just knowing his naked, soaked body is on the opposite side to me is enough to get my imagination run wild.

I can hear soft moans coming from him once the water hits his body, and that is enough to send a pulse to my cock.

I scrub myself off from the sweat I built up from my workout. The coolness of the water puts me in a relaxing state of calm. It's a nice way to ease myself after hearing the energetic pumping music when I was in the gym area.

I tilt my head up and let the water hit my face and feel the strands of water tingle down from my neck to the small of my back. I continue to scrub myself, but now I focus on my lower body.

With my hand movements and the sensual sounds coming from Mark, my cock begins to grow and harden. This is so not what I need right now. I am almost finished with my shower, and I do not want Mark to see my erection, and especially not other men who may show up in the changing room. *Fuck.*

I can cover myself with my towel that is hanging over the cubicle wall, but shit, I just have to shower for a few more moments, and hope my cock goes back to being soft. I never thought I would want my cock to go soft.

"Are you almost done, Kyle?" I hear Mark's voice cut through the impact of the water landing near me. He must have finished showering.

"Yeah, almost," I shout. "Are you done?"

"Yep. I'm just getting changed now."

"Ok. I'll be out in a min."

"There's no rush," he says, and that strikes me as odd. He has never said such a thing before when we hit the showers.

A few minutes pass and after washing my hair longer than I normally do, I finish up and pace myself back to my bag on the changing room bench, right where Mark is. He's already got his shorts on and is tying the laces on his trainers by the time I am next to him.

"You took a bit longer than usual in there," he nods to the back where the showers are at. "Did something come up?"

A cheeky growing smirks forms across his face. It's obvious what he is getting at.

"Yes actually. Something came up." I smirk back down at him whilst I dry myself up with my towel.

"I knew it. Well, I'll be honest. Something also came up for me," he reveals.

"You know we're alone. There's no one else here. You can just say you got a semi going on," I tell him.

"Yeah, but someone could pop in any moment. Plus, it feels more exciting and dirtier when we talk about it in secret like this."

"I agree with you, it does." As soon as I tell him that, I notice he lowers his eyes down to my groin, which is level with his head as he currently sits on the bench.

"You're becoming so obvious now," I say playfully.

"Well, I'm not trying to be sneaky here." He lets out a small laugh and I continue to dry myself off and put my regular clothes back on.

A few minutes later, and I am back to being fully clothed. We head out of the changing room, just as a group of men come in.

"Good timing. We got to have our sexual innuendos with no one else being present," he says upon entering the hallway.

"I know. It's almost like we should have spoken directly and drop the innuendos," I gleefully say.

"Oh, aren't you such a killjoy?"

Mark turns his gaze towards me as we exit the building. It's like he wants the reassurance that I am still with him. That I am still by his side. I think that's a sweet and wonderful thing. It's something he's always done since we became friends, but this time it feels different. I think we have both come out of the gym feeling more confident in going forward as something more than friends. The sexual innuendos, the flirting, and the chemistry between us, has risen to a new level from just the past hour and half at the gym. I am sure that would not have happened if neither one of us felt comfortable with the prospect of going forward in our relationship.

We turn round the corner of the building, and head to my car since I picked him up today, so I will drop him off back at his place.

"I feel so good after that. That was such a good workout," Mark's voice fills through the car just as we both seat ourselves.

"Yeah, same here. I haven't had a good workout like that for some time now. I feel so pumped up," I tell him.

A moment of silence cuts through the space between us and I take a few seconds longer than I should have to realise that I have been starting blankly at him, but I noticed he is doing the same thing to me.

"Mark, I-."

"Think we should talk," he finishes my sentence.

"Yeah," I mumble.

"I thought so. I was going to say the same." His eyes flicker at mine and I can see a moment of vulnerability through him. He's opening up to me and I do not want to mess this up.

"Mark, I am ready to take this further. Whatever this is," I motion my finger between him and myself. "But only if you're ready to. We both have to want this."

"I want this, Kyle. I have done for some time now. You know that."

He places his hand on my leg, and a quick burst of butterflies rush through my body.

Damn, Mark. I want you so badly.

"Sorry," he blushes and removes his hand. "Was that too much? I don't want to rush things."

"No, that was fine. In fact, I really liked it." I can tell that I am now blushing, too.

A warm and soft smile forms on his face and that only exaggerates the butterflies in my stomach even more.

"We've already kissed before," I say slowly, "so I was thinking we could move onto... blowjobs."

"What?" He blurts out. His eyes widen in shock.

"Is that too much?" I ask.

"Erm... I'm not sure." He inhales deeply and sits further back on the passenger seat. "A blowjob?" He questions and gazes at me.

"Yeah. I would like both of us to take turns. Only fair."

I can see my words have still left him in shock.

"And here's me, worrying about kissing you again would be too fast."

"You thought about kissing me?"

"I did. Have done so since our first kiss," he reveals. "Though now I am thinking about kissing your cock."

"Either sounds good to me. The cock kissing will have to wait for another time, since we are still in my car at the gym parking lot," I say to him.

"True, but we could kiss normally, right?"

I lean forward and plant my lips over his. The soft touch of his lips mushes against mine, and it puts me in a state of pure joy. A kind of joy I haven't felt since he last kissed me.

I place a hand at the back of his head, pulling him closer to me, with my other hand resting on his thigh. A second later and he does the same thing to me.

"Mmm... I've missed this," he breaks away and comes back onto my lips.

"Me too," I say and continue kissing his sweet lips.

After what must feel like the longest minute in our lives, we both pull away at the same time.

"That was... good. Really fucking good," he says in a sweet tone. "I hope you kiss me like that again."

"Oh, I will. Don't you worry about that."

We look at each blankly one more time and then I focus and pull out of the car park and head back to his place.

I feel so much better about taking things further with him. I know he feels the same. His wide cheeky grin across his face tells me so.

Chapter 21
Mark

"Well, you certainly seem happy," my dad says from across the living room as I enter the house. He's right. I can feel the sense of joy oozing out of me since Kyle kissed me.

"I'm just really happy, is all. I just had a great workout at the gym with Kyle. He just dropped me off now."

"I thought I saw his car drive past. Do you want a brew? I just boiled the kettle a few seconds before you popped in."

"Yeah, go on. A cup of coffee after a workout, is always a good thing."

He paces to the kitchen, and that's when I hear my mum walking down the stairs. I can always tell who is walking on the stairs. Everyone in this house seems to have their own foot pattern. It's something I've naturally picked up on over the years living in this house.

"Hi. Did you enjoy your workout today?" She asks me, followed by a cheerful smile.

"I did. I enjoy every workout with Kyle."

"It's nice that you two make such good workout buddies." She makes her way to the kitchen. "Good idea to have a workout a few days before the big match. Get your body loose for it."

ON THE PITCH

A flash of disappointment hits me as her talk about the match sends my mind to the last practice session. What a shitshow that turned out to be towards the end. It just had to be the last session, too. The most important one of all.

Unfortunately, since we haven't resolved the issue, I don't see us playing well as a team. But all of that isn't enough to take me out of my jovial mood. I just got kissed by my sexy best friend and we're taking things forward between us. Nothing can ruin that for me.

"Here you go." My dad hands me my coffee mug.

"Cheers, dad."

The heat emitting from the mug warms my hand and my bottom lip as I take my first sip. "Nice as always," I say to him. He makes the best coffee in this house. Better than my mum's coffee, yet they use the same brand. I don't get how his coffee is better, but it simply is.

"Are you nervous about the match?" My father asks me.

"I am. Probably more so since our last training session," I answer.

"Why is that?" My mother questions.

"Oh, I don't know. It just didn't feel like it was as productive as it should have been. With it being the last session and all before the match."

I don't tell them the real reason it wasn't a good session. I don't want them to worry about Kyle, since there isn't anything to worry about, and I don't want them to know about us yet. Not that anyone on the team knows about me and Kyle, but the fewer people know, the better. Me and Kyle will make it known to our friends and family when we're ready. For now, we are keeping it a secret until we are further into this new dynamic between us. Until we both declare ourselves as... boyfriend and boyfriend.

Damn. That feels so odd to think of us as boyfriends, yet it feels so right.

I enjoy the secrecy of us getting closer. It adds to the excitement. No one else knows about us, except for Sarah. I know she won't tell anyone else. She's been a good friend to me over the years, and more so to Kyle.

I sit myself down at the kitchen table and place my mug of coffee on a grey coaster after taking another sip from it.

It's then I check my messages from Kyle, and I notice I have a new unread message from him.

Kyle: Hey. My parents are out of the house for the entire night. So I've got the house to myself. That means I'll be all alone. I could sure use some company.

He sends me a wink emoji and follows up with another set of emojis that leave nothing to the imagination in relation to what we discussed in his car at the gym.

"Fuck," I calmly whisper to myself. Tonight? He wants to take things forward tonight?

Before I even reply, he sends a photo my way, and I am shocked and excited at the same time to receive such an image.

My eyes fixate on the clear picture of his hardening bulge peeking through his red boxers that are tightly wrapped around him.

Now I'm getting hard myself from just looking at it.

"What are you smirking at?" My dad questions. His words send a pulse of urgency through me for a moment.

"Oh, it's just a meme one of the lads on the team sent me. It's about one of the video games we play." I give my answer quickly. Hoping it will be enough to deter him from this situation.

ON THE PITCH

"I hear video games and I immediately lose interest," he laughs.

"As usual," I gently laugh back, and he makes his way upstairs.

Having that interaction with him just now, has me made glad that I didn't open my messages with Kyle in the kitchen moments ago. My mum or dad may have seen the photo I have received.

With being the only person in the kitchen, now that both my mum and dad have gone upstairs, I shift my focus back onto replying to Kyle.

I go to type something out, but I pause as I stare blankly at the photo again. With each second looking at it, I feel my cock twitch inside my jeans.

Mark: Fuck. I can't believe you sent me that. Your bulge looks amazing, by the way. I'm getting hard myself thanks to you.

Excitement and nerves course through me after I send my text. Never would I have thought that we would be messaging stuff like this, yet here we are doing so, and it feels so good.

Mark: I'll be round later and take care of that erection of yours.

I send him a wink emoji and, of course, the egg plant one too.

A fresh wave of adrenaline flows through me, but this time it's because of my declaration that I will suck him off later.

I can't believe we're really going to be doing this.

Kyle: Good, but don't worry. I also plan on sucking you off too. See you later.

Mark: Fucking nice.

I simply reply.

I finish my coffee and tell my parents I'll be staying at Kyle's tonight. It's not out of the usual, as we have stayed over at each other's houses many times before.

MICHAEL MABEL

Tonight, me and my best friend are taking things forward, and I am very much looking forward to it.

Chapter 22

Kyle

DING!

I hear the doorbell, and I try my best to hold in my excitement and nerves, knowing what is about to happen.

Slowly, I open the front door and see Mark and his cute smile. His eyes beam brightly at me, and I feel myself become weak in the knees from just seeing him already.

"Hey," he mumbles.

"Come on in." I nod my head back and watch him step foot inside the house.

After I close the door, I slowly walk to him. I remain locked on to his eyes with mine with every step I take. Neither of us says a word as we draw closer together.

Mark gently wraps his arms around my back. Pulling me in close until I am near his lips. I slowly graze his neck with my hands, and that's when we go in for our second kiss of the day.

It's only been a few hours since our kiss in my car at the gym parking lot, but to me, it feels much longer than that. I have become addicted to his lips. To his taste. His touch. I want more of whatever this is between us.

"You're such a good kisser," he whispers to me.

"So are you," I tell him.

Gently, I remove one hand from his neck and slowly grasp his bulge through the fabric of his jeans.

"Fuck," he breathes out. "You sure want this, don't you?" He smirks.

"You know I do." I smirk back in between our kiss.

For a moment, we continue our kiss. Neither one of us wants to let go, even though we both really want to do the next thing we have discussed.

Realising that myself, I pull back and a place a finger on his lips.

Understandably, he looks puzzled, but I know he's going to like what he sees next.

Quickly, I take off my dressing gown and reveal my half naked body. Showing the tight red boxers that I sent him a photo of a few hours earlier.

"Fuck me!" He exclaims.

"In time, yes, I will. But tonight is all oral stuff."

He quickly darts his eyes to mine after my joke. We haven't discussed full on sex yet. Only oral. But I'm sure we're both thinking of it.

"Do you like?" I tentatively say as I cusp my bulge.

"Absolutely," he declares.

"Well," I kiss him on the lips, "follow me."

I pace myself up the stairs, slowly. With each step I take, I purposely flex the muscles in my ass, knowing that's what he's looking at as he stares up from behind me.

"Are you enjoying the view back there?"

ON THE PITCH

"Oh, you tease. You fucking know I am. Fuck, Kyle. Your ass is amazing."

We arrive at the door to my bedroom, and I push it open.

"You first," I tell him. "You saw the back of my ass. Only fair I get to see yours in those tight jeans of yours."

He taunts me with a cherry blossom smile, "Fair enough" and he steps forward to the centre of my bedroom.

"Another reason I wanted you to come in first was so I could do this."

I gently push him onto my bed. His reaction goes from surprise to pleasure within a couple of seconds.

"You're really loving this, aren't you?" He says to me.

"I sure am," I respond and plant myself on his lap. Positioning my knees to the side of his legs and I clutch his head for another kiss.

I feel his arms wrap around my waist. The touch of his muscles sends a shock of pleasure through me. It's electrifying what I am feeling right now, and I know for sure that only he has this effect on me. No other man or person can make me feel this way.

With me still being positioned on his lap, I remove my hands from his head and slowly graze the sides of his shirt. Reaching for the bottom of the fabric, I swiftly pull his shirt over his head and toss it on the floor beneath my bed.

"I am a lucky man. This is the second time today I've seen your chest," I say in a soothing tone to my voice.

"You perv," he jokingly says.

Softly stroking his chest, his pecs, and his round muscular shoulders, has me reaching a new height of pleasure I have never felt before.

I realise I need to skip right to the real fun stuff, otherwise I may not hold out much longer.

"Move up the bed," I instruct as I stand back on the bedroom floor.

By using the muscles on his back and hands, I watch Mark move upward to my pillow. He settles himself on top of the duvet and watches me move on him with lust in his eyes. I've never seen him look at me like that before, but now that I have, I want to see this horny look from him many more times.

I place myself below his torso, with my knees placed at the side of his legs.

I edge my hands up his thighs and unbuckle his belt.

"Fuck, Kyle. I can't believe this is really happening." He breathes out heavily after speaking.

"We can stop if you want to. We can back out of this at any point if either of us becomes uncomfortable," I tell him.

"I'm more than ready for this, Kyle. Are you?"

"Of course I am. Now, let's see this hard cock of yours." I beam a bright smile at him.

"Fuck. I'm still in disbelief," he utters.

The tingling sounds coming from his belt buckle tickle my ears, as I loosen the belt around his waist.

"I've got that," I hear Mark tell me, and he swipes his belt out through his jeans and drops it on the floor. All that's left is for me to do is pull his jeans down, which I begin to do with glee.

Within seconds, I swipe his jeans down to his ankles, along with his boxers and place them beneath my bed.

"Oh, wow. Mark. It's so... so thick," I admit, with a tone of shock to my voice but also with a shaky rasp, as he may be too much to handle for my first time.

"I'm glad to hear that," he laughs. A big smirk forms across his face and I so badly want to kiss it off of him.

"Go as slow as you feel you need to, Kyle. Don't push yourself, for my sakes." My heart melts inside for him. Even when in a moment like this, he's still focusing on my comfort. Just like a good friend always does.

"Thanks. Now let's begin." I smirk back at him.

I gently wrap my right hand around his shaft and stroke it up and down a few times. With my other hand, I place it on his right thigh so that I can balance myself as I lower myself back down to his groin area.

Mark still has that lust in his eyes from moments ago. Having him look at me like that makes me even more excited, and more eager to please him.

I stop stroking him and instead, hold his stiff cock upwards, so it points towards my bedroom ceiling. I place my head closer to his groin and, with one swoop, I lick the underside of his shaft from the bottom to the tip.

"Oh... fuck," I hear him say. Deep breaths escape through his lips.

"Shit, Kyle. That felt so good," he gleefully says.

"I haven't even begun the sucking part yet. It's nice to know I'm off to a great start." I pull back my tongue and wrap my lips around his cock. First, I lower my head halfway down him. I would like to go further, but I am not ready for the whole thing yet.

With my mouth halfway down his dick, I slowly bob my head back and forth.

"Umph... ugh," he groans lightly. "Oh, that feels good."

I wink at him as an acknowledgment of his words.

The longer this act between us carries on, the more relaxed and at ease I become.

By having this intimate moment between the both of us, I already feel closer to him than I have ever before. Our naked bodies laid open for each other to see in my bedroom. A room we have spent so much time in together as friends. Whether it was playing video games, board games, talking about football and many other things.

Now I will have a fresh memory of us in my room. A memory that will bring pleasure for sure, but also joy, as my bedroom is now the setting of the first time, we became intimate like this. Of when we pushed things forward between us and moved beyond from best friends to something more.

"Shit, you're fucking good at this," I hear Mark praising me. "How did you learn to become so good at this?"

"I've watched a lot of videos," I giggle and continue pleasing him.

I notice one of his hands beside me, so I lightly hold his wrist and guide his hand to rest on the back of my head.

"You're really into this more than I thought you'd be," he says.

I look deep into his eyes and lower my lips to the bottom of his shaft. The first time I've gone that far down on him.

"Oh, fuck!" He exclaims.

With his hand guiding my head, I pick up the pace.

"Mmm... umph," my groans escape me.

I press my lips more tightly around his cock and apply more pressure to the underside of his shaft with my tongue, all the while bobbing my head back and forth much quicker than before.

"Oh, shit Kyle. I'm close. I'm-."

Suddenly, the contents of his orgasm fill up inside my mouth.

"Argh, FUCK!" He shouts. Pleasure and ecstasy now take a hold over him.

His cock continues to pump more rounds of his cum deep inside my mouth. The taste of it settles on my tongue.

This taste is new to me, and it has levelled up the sense of enjoyment I am receiving right now.

"Oh... ugh, yeah," Mark breaths out. His breath is becoming shallower, and I can feel the supply of his cum slowing down.

With his climax now finished, I take in the remaining drops of his cum, and look him deep in his eyes with a smile on my face, and swallow all that he pumped inside of me.

"Fuck!" His beautiful eyes widen in surprise. "I was not expecting you to swallow."

"Really? I was always going to swallow. I wouldn't want it all to go waste now," I say in a flirtatious tone.

"I bet you want me to swallow, too."

"Only if you want to," I reply as I straighten myself above his legs and take off my boxers.

"I sure do." Enthusiasm seeps through his voice.

The brown irises of his eyes lower down from my head to my cock, and judging by his smile, I know he likes what he sees.

"Damn, your cock is thick."

"I'm glad you like what you see." I playfully tease him by slowly edging towards him on my knees. "With all that excitement at sucking you off, I don't think I'll last long right now." My groin is now right in front of his face. "I am ready to bust."

"I'm more than ready. C'mon. Give me all you've got." He smirks up at me.

"Open up," I instruct as I look down at his head resting on my bed pillow.

With his mouth now open, I slowly thrust my dick inside of his mouth. My knees keep me steady as the tantalising feel of his lips and tongue around my shaft causes my legs to shake.

"Oh, fuck Mark. I'm close." As soon as my words leave my mouth, he licks my dick inside of his mouth. Almost as he is testing me.

With one final pump, I bust my load right at the back of his throat. My pent-up orgasm exploding all of its contents in him.

"Ohhh... fuck. Argh." I groan loudly and close my eyes. Taking in this moment with Mark.

I open my eyes and look down at Mark. "Did you enjoy that?" I ask and pull my now softening cock out of his mouth.

Before he answers, he looks up at me and swallows what I left inside of him. "I sure did."

Our eyes lock on each other for a moment. Taking in what just happened between us. Of what we just did.

"That was fun," I say with glee, and I move over him and settle by his side.

"That sure was, bestie." We both laugh and he places his arm around my neck.

Our bare-naked bodies are side by side with each other. Something I never thought would happen, but I sure am happy it is.

I nudge into his arm and rest a hand over his chest, feeling his pecs heave in time with his slow breathing.

ON THE PITCH

"This was perfect, Mark." He turns to me with an innocent look. "It sure was, Kyle. It sure was."

Chapter 23
Mark

"I still can't believe we just did all of that," I say to Kyle, with his head resting near my chin. His hand softly stroking my pecs. The tender touch of his bare flesh feels new to me. I feel a pull towards him now. Ready to share another powerful moment with him.

"Yeah, me too. That was fucking fantastic."

"Best way to put it," I iterate. "I can't believe I just sucked my best friend's cock. Never would have thought I would say that."

"The look on your face when I swallowed was priceless. That was a treat to see," he says.

He nudges his head and looks at me with his ocean blue eyes.

Seeing him like this, after experiencing our first intimate moment together, feels different. I still see him as my best friend in life. That will never change. But now I see something more than I ever did before. I see us growing closer more than either of us thought possible. Our bond with each other, expanding. Reaching new heights, the further we take this new relationship.

"You are so cute," I tell him, and gently caress his cheek.

"Awe, getting all gushy on me now," he jokes.

"When I have my sexy best friend lying next to me naked after sucking each other off, then yeah, I am going to get 'gushy'."

"Mark," his use of my name with a bare tone tells me that whatever he is going to say next is serious. "Do you think it's time we officially become boyfriends?"

I pull my head back so that I can get a better view of his face, as this conversation requires focus.

"It has been on my mind, Kyle. I've just been unsure of how to bring the subject up."

"Do you want to call each other 'boyfriend'?" He raises his chest off the bed to direct his question at me, and with a smile on my face, looking back at him, I say, "Of course I want to be boyfriends."

My answer gets him to smile back at me and his cheeks turn rosy red.

He seals my lips with a kiss and quickly pulls back to say, "That was the correct answer. Boyfriend," and he lies beside me like he did moments ago.

I tuck my arm under his neck again, and he lays his hand over my chest just like before.

"Are you nervous about tomorrow?" I ask of him. We haven't discussed the upcoming match since I arrived at his house.

"I am. Are you?"

"Yeah, me too. Though I don't think I would be if our last practice session had gone smoothly," I say.

"That's why I am nervous. I'm worried about how we're gonna play tomorrow with the rest. I don't think I would worry as much if we had discussed what happened with the rest. Mainly with Jake."

Kyle's tone may be cool and collected, but I know him well. I can sense that he is worrying about this more than he lets on.

"I understand, and you're right. I think we both would go into the match in a much better frame of mind if we had talked with the other lads, but don't worry. You've got me. I've always got your back."

He soothes his hand from my right pec over to my left, where my heart is, and pats on my muscle.

"I know," he smiles. "And I have always got your back, too."

I caress my hand through his hair and taste his lips one more time for tonight.

"Goodnight, my boyfriend," my voice is soft.

"Goodnight to you too, boyfriend," he says in a sombre tone, and with that, I am staying at his place for the night. Ready for tomorrow's game.

Chapter 24
Kyle

Today's the day of the big game. The last match of the season. Us against the lads from Manchester. The Majestic Lions vs The Blue Hearts. They're good from what I've heard.

"You ready, my sexy boyfriend?" I still can't believe I can now call Mark, my boyfriend. Every time I say it, my chest feels lighter than air. I'm on cloud nine because of him.

"I am, sweet cheeks," he quips. "Are you?" His look of concern for me is touching and makes me weak in the knees for him. If we had time and some privacy, I'd get on my knees and repeat what I did to him last night, but that will hopefully happen later, after the match.

"I am ready. I feel much better about the game after our talk last night," I answer.

"Same here."

We both pace ourselves over to the other players on our team, and it's then we notice our parents and his sister, gathered together at the bench area, along with the other spectators.

The walk to the rest of our team is nothing but awkward. None of us have spoken to each other since the incident that happened at our last training session before today's match.

Mark and I woke up to a message this morning from Jason, our captain. It was nice to read that he apologises for not communicating with us any earlier.

Speaking of which, I see him making his way to us. Meeting halfway before we join the rest.

"Fellas. I know I texted you both, but I want to apologise in person, especially before kick-off. So, again. I'm sorry for not getting in touch any sooner about what happened at the last training session."

"Apology accepted," Mark declares.

"It's all good," I say to Jason.

"That's good to hear, lads," Jason says, and shakes our hands. "Though I wouldn't count on getting an apology from Jake before we start. He's being very stubborn."

"Oh, don't worry. I wasn't counting on that," I respond.

"Kyle, I just want to say before we start, that to be honest, I wasn't too sure how to speak with you. Hearing what Jake was saying on that day, I wasn't sure on how to act as captain in that situation."

"It's fine, Jason. Thanks for apologising. I appreciate it."

"Cheers. Now let's go play and smash this," Jason exclaims and struts over to the rest of the team, and we follow him from behind.

We all take a few minutes to greet each other and converse about the match that's about to be played.

As the conversation in the group circle flows, the lads on the Manchester team walk by and kindly greet us. They all introduce themselves, and we do the same.

One of them catches my eye, not just because he is fit as fuck, which I'm sure Mark agrees with, but also because I think I've seen him on social media before, promoting Manchester's gay village.

ON THE PITCH

I mentally make a note to see to speak with him after the match. I'm curious if he is the person I have in mind of when I saw him.

"Players, get into position!" The referee shouts out loud for all of us to hear, and every player gets into position.

As a defender, I position myself near to our goal.

I turn my head and give a nod to our goal keeper, Stephen. He nods back and gives me a big thumbs up. It's comforting to see him be in a positive mood. He plays an important role, and I have a feeling he will be very busy during this game.

With my focus now back on what's in front of me, I notice Mark looking over my way. A soft, cute smile beams across the distance between us. A smile that comforts me and tells me I can lean on him for support.

I wink at him, which causes him to break his lips apart, and his small, cute smile turns into a big, wide grin.

Instinctively, we both look ahead to the referee and see Jason meeting the other team's captain in the centre of the pitch.

With a blow of the whistle from the referee, the game starts and adrenaline courses through me suddenly, which is likely the case for every other player on the field.

Jason gets the first kick, and passes the ball to Mark, which is a good play, as Mark is one of our best strikers.

Mark doesn't waste the opportunity given to him, as he rushes over to the other team's side of the pitch and the rest of us try our best to keep up with him.

"Over here," Tony shouts from Mark's left, and Mark shoots the ball across to the left side. Tony stops the ball with his heel, and dashes forward, cutting through the defence of the other team.

"Nice pass," I shout over to Mark. I think it's important I show him my support during the match. I believe this will help boost morale, and not just between us, but also amongst the rest of our team when they hear our call outs. Though, I'm not sure how effective my call outs will be. I am getting an 'iffy' vibe from some of the other players on my team. It's as if they feel awkward to be around me. That would explain why some of them were trying to avoid eye contact with me, when Mark and I first arrived.

It's no surprise at all that Jake is the most reluctant to look at me, speak to me, or even be near me. For the sake of us winning the match, he could at least tolerate being near me for passes. It's vital we all work together as a team.

Within moments of receiving the ball from Mark, Tony shoots the ball after passing through the other team's defence and scores the first goal of the game.

"Woo!" Tony shouts and punches the air in a moment of celebration, all whilst he rushes to the centre to meet the rest of us.

"Well in, Tony," Jason says and high fives him.

"Nice one lad," I hear Mark say to him, as we all gather in a closed circle.

"Nice scoring," I tell Tony and gently fist bump him.

After a brief moment of celebration, we all get back to our positions. Ready to continue the game.

Ten more minutes go by with no progress made from either team. Though I can tell that the fellas from Manchester seem much more determined than before, ever since Tony scored our first goal. They have pushed us back and got close to our defence, and even tried for a couple of goals. One of their shots bounced off the goal post itself and the other, our goal keeper Stephen, saved, thankfully.

"Pass it to me," I hear one of the other team's players shout, and his teammate kicks the ball his way. Once the player who made the call has received the ball, he dashes his way forward, cutting through gaps between my teammates that are near him.

"Jake, get in the centre and block him," I advise. My voice is loud enough for Jake to hear, but he doesn't listen. Instead, he gives me a glare that tells me he's annoyed with my call out, and whilst he's glaring at me and ignores my advice, the other team's striker cuts through our defence and scores their first goal.

"Shit!" I hear Jason, our captain, mutter. The rest of my team share the same sentiment.

We are no longer winning. It's now tied.

Fuck!

Just what is his problem with me? Jake's attitude might cost us the game.

I take a moment to decompress and focus.

Mark looks over at me and shows me a look of concern. He seems to know something is up without me telling him. It's like the closer we become with each other, the more we're in sync. It's like an invisible tether connects our hearts. My soul attached to his. Wherever I go.

It's now the afternoon, and the sun is beaming brighter than it had when the match started in the morning.

The score is still one to one, and after a very much needed break during halftime, which allowed me to relax and focus, the second half of the match is underway.

Tony and Jason push forward, trying to steal a chance at reclaiming possession of the ball. The both of them near the opposing player who has the ball, and it is Tony who comes out of that scuffle successfully, as he dashes to the side with the ball beneath him.

But his fortunate luck only goes so far, as the player who I recognise on the Manchester team cuts through and takes the ball off Tony and shoots the ball towards our goal.

I turn my gaze to follow the trajectory of the ball, hoping it misses the goal or Stephen catches it. But alas, none of those two things happen.

The rousing applause and cheers erupts from the other team as they celebrate their second goal of the game.

The scoring player runs back to his teammates, all of whom open their arms out ready, and pull him in for a group hug.

"Fuck yeah," I hear one of them shout towards the sky. Fist bumping the air, too.

The referee blows his whistle, and that's it. The game is over. We lost. They won.

Chapter 25

Kyle

"Hey," Mark sweetly says to me. He places his arm around my neck and tugs me in closer. "We did good. You did good, especially. I'm proud of you, babe."

"Thanks. You were great out there, too. Seeing you run in those shorts of yours has got me going," I tell him.

"Geez, the match has just finished and you're already talking like this. I never knew you were such a horny fuck."

Seeing him being his usual funny self, quickly puts me in a better mood.

His jokes, his words, and his laugh. Everything about him is like a medicine to me. He always makes me feel better and brighter. No matter how bad I may feel.

"I'm glad we've got each other, Mark. I'm very lucky to have you in my life."

"No, Kyle. I'm the lucky one." His sweet innocent glare clutches my heart. I so badly want to kiss him right now, but I certainly won't do that while the other players are around us.

"Speaking of luck, though, how about I get lucky with you tonight?" He whispers. His words tingle not only my ears but also my dick. Damn, he better not give me an erection right now.

"Talking like that with other people around us. Now, who's the horny fucker?" I lightly laugh and smile at him.

Our faces pull closer to each other the longer we talk. It's like we're magnets to each other. Drawing the other one into our own personal space of gravity.

Not wanting to cause any ruckus, I stop myself and show him a glare, with my eyes wide momentarily, to show the alertness I feel within myself.

Mark catches on and pulls back to, and that's when I notice Jason, Tony, among a few others, approach us.

"Hey, guys. Disappointing result, I know, but it's not the end of the world," Jason says. Throwing his hands in the air, in a motion of defeat. "You lads have improved so much. From your dribbling with the ball and taking shots. I'm impressed. Good work, you two."

"Cheers, Jason," Mark says back to him.

"Yeah, that means a lot. So, thanks," I tell him.

Mark and I converse with the lads, all except for Jake, for a post-game talk. Breaking down what we did right, and what went wrong.

I know what went wrong, and it's something that if it hadn't happened, we would all be feeling much better right now. And that's if Jake had simply listened to my call and got the ball off the opposing player, who was rushing towards us and prevented their first goal. At least that way we would have come to a draw, and maybe win on penalties.

At some point, I am going to have to speak to Jake, one on one.

ON THE PITCH

I seriously need to know what his fucking issue is with me. It's driving me nuts, and it has now cost us a game too. The last match of the season. Of all games, it had to be this one.

After conversing with the rest of the team, Mark and I head on over to the side of the pitch to meet our families.

"Hey, sweetie. I'm sorry you guys didn't get the win, but don't get too worked over it." My mum comforts me. With her arm around my neck, she pulls me and kisses me on the cheek. "I'm so proud of you," she tells me.

"You did good, son. We're both proud of you," my dad follows up with his words. His face says it all, that he is indeed full of pride for me.

"Thanks, you two." I tell the both of them and we come in for a big family hug.

I see some of my uncles, aunts and cousins are here too, along with Sarah.

In their own time, they all say similar things to what my mum and dad said before.

I glance over to my right and see Mark have his moment with his family. His parents, Rebecca, and Peter, being as cheerful and prideful as my parents are for me. It's great that we both have supportive families to lean on and count on. Whether that be for the small things in everyday life, or the big things, like coming out as gay.

We all engage in further conversation and enjoy the refreshments that the organisers have provided for both the players and spectators.

The conversation is easy-going, as my extended family knows Mark and his family well.

"Hey, babe," Mark whispers to me from my side. We're only a few feet away from some of our family members and him calling me 'babe' so close to them, causes urgency to pulse through me, as none of them know about us. But him calling me that, feels sweet and naughty. His words and cheeky smile, along with the sweat off his football kit, make me want to rush back to mine or his, and have our way we each other. Rip our clothes off and go at it fully for the first time together.

"Hey, sexy," I reply. "You know I'm starting to really like it when you call me babe."

"I already knew that. Yours lips give it away."

"How so?" I question.

"They slowly curl upwards. You try your best to suppress it, but your smile always wins. And please, Kyle. Don't suppress your joy. It's always a pleasure seeing you smile."

"Since when did you become such a sweet talker?"

"That's easy." He nudges his head closer to my ear. "Since I fell in love with my best friend."

He pulls his head back and our eyes lock on to each other, and I feel like my heart is doing back flips after hearing him talk so passionately like that.

The emotions I feel within myself turn and twist inside my chest. With every word Mark speaks to me with such a loving tone, makes me fall in love with him more than I thought possible. I can't get enough of this man, and I don't think I ever will.

Realising how close we've become and how sure we are of us being together, and having our families with us right now, makes me so desperately want to tell them about us. Just get the secret out now so that we can be more open about the two of us.

ON THE PITCH

I swing my arm around Mark's shoulder and pull him in close to me.

"There's something I want to ask you about" My voice is quiet as I guide us away from the rest, but not too far to raise some eyebrows.

"Yeah, what is it you want to talk about?" His voice now matches my hushed tone.

"How do you feel about telling our families about us right now?"

His eyebrows dart upwards on his face, signalling to me his surprise reaction.

"What! You want to do this now? With the other lads on our team just on the other side of the pitch. What if they come over and hear about us being a couple?"

I feel myself smiling so damn fucking hard at his last couple of words.

"What's with the smile?" He asks.

"You called us a couple. It still amazes me we are now a couple."

"It still is pretty shocking," he says.

"But back to what you were saying about the team and, honestly, I don't care. I think most of them would be okay with us. Maybe not Jake, though. But besides, we have our families right here. We've got all the support we need."

I wear my emotions on my sleeve now, the more I talk to Mark. I hold him by the wrists as I try to convince him.

With a quick glance, I see our families are still gabbing to each other. Paying no mind to me and Mark. The only one who has noticed us is our friend Sarah.

She looks over at me and simply smiles my way. Her bright soul piercing through. Something about her facial expression tells me she knows me and Mark are discussing something very important.

"You're right. Let's do this. Let's tell them about us." Mark's words cause a wave of happiness to rise through me. My hands shake, and I feel my lips stretch wide across my face.

"Come on then. Let's go tell them all," he says.

We casually walk back to the others.

Mixed emotions of nervousness and excitement course through me with every step we take.

"Nervous?" I ask him.

"Yep. Are you?"

"I am."

He brushes up even closer to me, and that's when I feel his hand reaching for mine. His fingers gently grip my hand.

"Don't worry. I've got you." His words calm my nerves, as well as his hand holding mine.

I look into his beautiful brown irises and see the soul of the man I love. The man who I can proudly call my boyfriend.

We get closer to the larger group, and I notice Sarah has now seen us holding hands. She smacks her hands together and her jaw hits the floor.

She knows what we're about to do.

"Everyone," I call out. "There is something Mark and I would like to tell you."

A second after I speak, all of them turn round to lay their eyes on me and Mark. And in unison, they all lower their gaze to where mine and Mark's hands meet.

ON THE PITCH

I see before me a range of emotions taking over them. Some of clear happiness, shock, and confusion. But I know these people will be supportive of us.

"W-what. When?" My mother barely gets her words out.

Mark's mum does the same, but I notice his dad Peter smiling right at Mark. It's a beautiful smile. One that shows he's happy for his son.

I look over to my dad and see that he is just as bewildered as the other family members are, but soon enough, everyone is beaming with happiness for me and Mark.

"When did you two get together?" Mark's mum, Rebecca, asks.

"Yes, please answer. We would all like to know," my mum interjects.

Me and Mark share a comical look with each other, as we can both tell our mums are very keen for the details. It's like they're both treating our story as something they would see on a TV drama. Meanwhile, our dads are still chilling behind them, taking sips from their beers.

Me and Mark spend the next few minutes filling in everyone who is curious on the details and answering questions.

After we wrap up our little Q&A session, we say bye to our families, as both our parents are out of town for the next day, and the other family members head on back home.

It's then I notice our team members from across the pitch with their families.

Jason waves, and we wave back. I see him getting ready to leave.

"I've just realised. Jason would definitely know about us now. He just saw us, and we're still holding hands," I point out.

"Oh, yeah. Well, now we know he's okay with us, since he just waved," Mark says.

"Yeah. That is good to know. Anyway, we should get going."

"Ooh, where should we go? We have a selection of two houses. My place, or yours? Since both our parents are out of town."

"Hmm," I wonder. "We've sucked each other off on my bed. So maybe now we do something fun on yours," I tell Mark.

"I like how you think, my sexy, beautiful boyfriend."

"You don't have to flatter me. You're already getting some tonight."

"I know, but can't a man keep flattering his boyfriend with compliments?"

"He sure can," I respond, and go in for a kiss.

Mark places his hands on my hips, and I hug him tightly. Our lips seal together, and I now realise this is the first time we have kissed at the pitch. A place where we have bonded and become closer by having deep conversations. It's also our first public kiss.

It's safe to say that we are definitely out to everyone now. But at this moment, it's just us. Me and him.

"Damn, I could do that forever," Mark says with a sexy gravel tone that just makes me want to pounce on him right now. Tear off his football outfit and go wild.

"Me too. Now let's go to yours, so that I can please my man," I say to him and plant a quick smooch on his cheek.

"Hey!" I hear someone shout.

I turn my head and look over to my left side, toward the sound of the voice I heard.

I see the man that I saw earlier, before the game started. A man who plays on the Manchester team and who looks familiar to me.

"Hello," he says to me and Mark, as he now stands next to us. "Sorry for abruptly shouting. My name is James."

ON THE PITCH

James smiles hard at us both and shakes our hands.

"Nice to meet you, James," Mark greets him.

"Yes. It's a pleasure to meet you. I think I recognise you from somewhere. Have you promoted the gay village in Manchester on social media? I think that is where I recognise you from?" I ask him.

"I have, and that is why I came over here to see you both."

For a second, I am left puzzled why he would come over here to see us, and judging by Mark's face, I think he is feeling the same as me.

"I should just tell you two right away," he laughs. "So, yes. I do volunteer sometimes to promote the gay village in Manchester and LGBT+ events that take place around that area. So recently, me and my team have been looking to interview LGBT+ players in sports. So, I saw you two having your moment just now, and I just had to take the chance to see if you both will be up for it."

"I am," I tell James. "But I would like to know more about it before I do the interview."

"Same here," Mark says.

"Good. I am happy to hear that."

I can see the happiness levels rise in James, after me and Mark have both taken an interest in what he has told us.

"It isn't a long interview. It's just a few questions about why you wanted to play the sport, how do you feel as gay, or bisexual men playing in a sport that has often been hostile to men who aren't straight. You can both send me a photo of you two wearing your team's uniform and we add the questions and answers to the side of your photos, and then post them on our page. So, does that sound like something you two are still interested in?"

"Sure. Count me in. This sounds fantastic," I tell him.

"I'll do it as well," Mark gives his answer.

"Great! That's wonderful to hear. The interviews are virtual. So you can do it at home at your convenience."

"Nice," Mark simply says.

We give James our social media handles and arrange a date for the interviews to be done and say bye to him.

"Can you believe it? In a matter of minutes, we have gone from telling our families, friends, team members about us, to now also agreeing to do an interview about being gay men playing football. Crazy." Mark speaks as we walk to my car. We both arrived in mine.

"I know. It's absolutely nuts. To be honest, all of this had made forget about us losing," I say.

"Same. Now you just mentioned nuts, and I so badly want to bust mine and yours tonight," he says with a cheeky grin to boot.

"Tonight is going to be fun. I can't wait to tear your football kit off," I tell him.

"I feel the same. I've been eyeing your ass nearly all day in those tight shorts of yours."

Mark slowly slides his hand from the small of my back to my ass cheek.

"You're so impatient. I bet you would like to do it in the car."

"You got that right. So why not?"

"We are not fucking in my car," I tell him.

"Why not?" He pouts.

"Well, for starters, we're still outside, in a public space. That alone should be enough. But also, I really can't be assed cleaning the mess up."

"There won't be a mess if you swallow again." His cheeky grin returns after saying that.

"Oh, you dirty horny fuck," I jokingly tease.

He grabs a hold of my hand and raises my knuckle to his mouth and kisses it.

"I love you," he tells me, and this is the second time he has told me so today.

"I love you too, Mark. I have done so for a very long time."

We reach my car and I drive us to his place. Ready for a night with my man.

Chapter 26
Mark

We arrive at my place after leaving the pitch. It's now late in the evening, and I am so glad to have the house to myself with Kyle. Tonight, we are taking things further. We're going all the way. And there is no other man I would want to do that with.

I lazily place my bag on the couch, and he does the same.

"I am fucking knackered," he tells me and slouches himself against my chest.

"I hope you're not too tired for tonight," I say. I look down into his blue, piercing eyes.

"I'm not tired enough for that. In fact, the thought of your naked body and cock, gets me energised."

"That is good to hear, Kyle."

I slowly guide his hand to my growing bulge. He feels the loose fabric of my shorts around my cock, and I can see the lust in his eyes.

"Oh, fuck. You're hard already?"

"Of course I am. I've got my handsome boyfriend right next to me."

He simply smirks as a response and lowers himself down, aligning his head next to my crotch.

"Mmm... Oh, baby. I've become addicted to this," he tells me, with his hand now firmly gripping my cock through the fabric.

Kyle then nudges his face firmly against my cock. Taking in the scent and feel of my sweat.

"Mmm," he moans.

He hasn't even begun sucking me off yet, and this is already becoming too much for me, and I do not want to cum yet. Tonight, I want to go full penetration.

"Oh, Kyle. Babe. This is too much for me. I'm gonna cum at this rate."

He slowly backs off and stands back up.

"Sorry. I guess I got too caught up in the moment. I know tonight we plan on going all the way through."

"Are you ready for it?" I ask him. I don't want to feel like he has to rush through things for me, but based on his enthusiasm for my dick, it's safe to say he may want this more than me.

"I am. Are you?"

"I am, Kyle."

"Good." He closes the gap between us and kisses me hard. His arms slide around my hips and his hands grip my ass cheeks. "It's time for this ass of yours to plough me."

"You've already deemed yourself the bottom for tonight. Did you ever think perhaps I want your cock to?" My voice is smooth, matching the same sexy vibe he has been teasing me with.

"You mean this?" He now guides my hand around his cock.

"Yes." I hum next to his ear.

"Perhaps another time. Besides, you've been checking my ass out all day. I know you want it," he teases, and turns around, sliding his ass up against my dick.

"Oh, fuck! Okay, seriously, we need to go to my bedroom now. I don't know how much longer I can take your sexiness."

He simply smiles. "Well, lead the way," he instructs me, and I pace myself out of the living and towards the stairs.

"Such a lovely sight to behold," I hear him from behind me on the stairs.

"You're just as much of an ass man like me," I tell him.

"Great minds think alike. Now, hurry. I am begging for your cock."

"Man, you really are a horny devil. I love it," I tell him.

We enter my bedroom, and just as I turn round to face Kyle, he pulls me towards him and fiercely kisses me.

This isn't a perfect, beautiful kiss you'd see at a wedding. This is a hot, passionate, wild kiss. A kiss that tells me he so desperately wants me and my cock right now, and I am more than happy to give myself to him.

I will always give all of me to him.

"Mmm, you smell so sexy." He growls underneath my chin as he now kisses my neck.

"I smell of sweat, babe," I say.

"Exactly. Sweat you've built up from playing footie. Working those muscles of yours. All of it is so sexy. Now it's time to see what you've got for me."

A devilish grin grows on his handsome face.

He lightly nudges me closer to the bed and then pushes me back.

I fall on my bed, and I see my man lay himself above my legs. That look of hunger and lust is still present in his eyes.

Quickly, he tugs my football shorts and boxers and pulls them off, causing my now hard cock to spring upwards.

"Fuck, Mark. You're so fucking hard."

"For you, Kyle. I always am."

"Let's get your dick nice and wet," he tells me, and then he takes in all of me in one go. His lips sealing shut around my shaft.

I feel his tongue licking the tip.

"Umph." His moans are just as enticing as his touch.

He bobs his head up and down, spreading his spit over my shaft. Getting it nice and wet, just like he said he would.

"Oh, fuck, Kyle. It's time," I tell him. "I need to fuck you right now."

He slowly eases off my dick and takes his football shirt off.

He's about to take off his shorts and boxer briefs, but I stop him. "No. Give me the pleasure of taking those off for you," I say.

"You're already going to get the pleasure of taking my ass. Isn't that enough?"

"With you Kyle. Nothing is ever enough."

His cheeks blush after he hears my words, and that makes my heart flutter.

I pull the drawer from my bedside cabinet and grab the bottle of lube and a condom.

"Nice to see you've come prepared. I brought my lube and condoms in case you didn't have any. They're in my bag," he tells me.

"I always come prepared. Now. Bend over," I say directly.

"Oh, well, aren't you such a gentleman? No foreplay at all."

"Kyle, seeing you run in those shorts during the game was enough foreplay for me. Even then, we were touching each other when we came inside the house and then you even sucked me off. How much more foreplay do you need?"

"Fair point. Now, get me ready, babe."

He eases himself forward and bends over. His ass now directly pointing to me. I lean closer to him and kiss the side of his neck, as I gently wrap my arms around him. The soft touch of our flesh touching each other calms my nerves.

Kyle nudges his head further back, leaning into my kiss.

"Mark. That feels so good. You feel so good." His voice is soft and relaxed. His tone soothes me and brings me into a relaxed state.

"Are you ready?" I ask him.

"I am."

"Okay then," and with his confirmation, I slowly drag his shorts and boxer briefs down to his ankles. He lifts his feet up so that I can pull the remaining clothing off him, which I do.

I pop open the small bottle of lube and begin spreading it around the centre of his ass.

"Ooooh," he moans. "That alone feels good."

"I'm glad you like that," I respond.

He arches his back to me, leaning more into my touch.

I motion my finger around the entry of his ass, applying the lube in a circular motion.

"Babe, I think that's enough now," Kyle tells me.

"Are you sure?"

"Yes."

"Well, I am still going to put some on my dick. I made sure to get lube that doesn't break condoms," I tell him.

"Always taking precaution," he quips.

"You know it."

ON THE PITCH

A few seconds later and I have put the condom on my dick, with the lube covering it from the base to the tip. This is mine and Kyle's first time with a man, so I want to be as gentle as possible.

I lightly place my hands on the side of his hips, with him now completely arching forwards.

Slowly, I ease my cock into him. The feeling of entering the man who I now get to call my boyfriend, is electrifying.

This new level of touch with him sends a shudder through me. I can't believe this is happening, but I am so glad it is.

"Ooh, ah," he moans.

"Are you alright?" I ask, feeling concerned. I am sure he can detect my worry for him in my voice.

"Yeah. I'm fine. Honestly. It's just new. That's all. I've done a lot practicing with a butt plug and dildo, yet I still feel stretched by you," he informs me.

"You've been practicing with a dildo and a butt plug? You didn't tell me."

"I wanted to surprise you. Anyway, are we really having a full-blown conversation whilst your dick is in me?"

"We sure are," I humorously say. "Anyway, back to the action."

A light, quiet laugh escapes his mouth after he hears my words, and it's so cute to hear him laugh like that.

With my hands still placed on his hips, I ease myself some more inside of him, and then slowly pull away, but not completely.

"That... that feels good," I hear him say, followed by a soft hum from his throat.

With his positive statement of my technique, I slowly pick up the pace.

"Ah, oh," Kyle continues to moan.

"Ugh!" I grunt. The sounds coming from Kyle are like musical notes to me. They tingle my ears and make me want to hear the song of his groans to continue.

Seeing him taking the pleasure that I am giving him is amazing. Knowing that I am the cause for his happiness right now. No one else but me. That brings me joy.

"How are you liking that?" I question.

"I'm fucking loving it. Keep at it," he answers.

"Gladly," I simply say, and I keep thrusting my cock inside of him. I am still keeping to the same pace I have been for the past few minutes, as to not cause him any discomfort.

I watch him lean upwards, with his back slowly making its way to me, and suddenly, Kyle is neck and neck with me. His back is now in contact with my chest, just like we were moments ago when I kissed his neck.

With Kyle now next to me, I slide my hand from his right hip to his dick and slowly stroke it.

"Fuck, Mark. You make me feel so good."

I simply acknowledge his words by going faster and pulling him closer with my left hand.

"Fuck," he grunts.

"I fuckin love hearing you like this," I tell him.

"You're the reason for it. I bet that turns you on. Doesn't it?"

I kiss his neck and say, "It sure does."

He leans more into me and slides a hand at the back of my head, holding me still for us to kiss once more.

ON THE PITCH

The mixed sounds of us kissing and our moans fill the space around my bedroom. There is nothing else to be heard except for the two of us.

"Mmm... umph."

"Damn, you moan so much," I tell him. "Don't change that. I love it."

"I can tell," he says with a hard smile. "I want you to be on top of me now."

"Are you sure?"

"Yes, Mark. I want to see your face when you finish."

"Okay then."

I gently pull out of him and move to the side of the bed so that he can position himself.

Kyle moves up to the top of my bed and lowers himself.

Before I get back near him, he tells me to wait, and I watch him pull out one of my pillows and he places it underneath the spot between his ass and lower back, for support.

"Good thinking," I tell him.

"I looked this up online."

"Do you mean an article about sex tips or porn?"

"Erm... both," he answers.

"Sure," I say with a sarcastic tone.

I place myself below him and grip my cock and guide it back inside of him.

He closes his eyes for a moment as he takes in the pleasure that I am giving him.

I take in the sight of his muscled, toned body, bare beneath me. All for my viewing pleasure.

We look deep into each other's eyes and then he wraps his legs around my waist, pulling me closer to him, which causes me to glide the entire length of my cock back inside of him.

"Get to it. Stud," he teases.

"Happy to." I blow him a kiss and thrust inside of him again.

The moans from the both of us return. This time louder and more aggressive than before, matching the faster pace I am going at. We are both more relaxed with this new dynamic between us. That dynamic being hot, magnificent sex with each other.

"Oh, fuck yes. This feels so good, Kyle."

"It does babe."

Kyle lays his arms out and reaches for my hands that are on the duvet beside his chest.

"Yeah... yes," he softly groans this time. "Mark, come closer."

I do as he says and lean further down to him. Our chests nearly touching one another.

"I have wanted this for so long," he reveals in between heavy breaths.

"Me too."

A moment passes by of us simply gazing into each other's eyes, all while I continue thrusting inside of him.

Quickly, he gently grips the back of my head and guides me closer to his mouth and seals my lips with a kiss.

As our kiss continues, he places his other hand on the side of my face, whilst his other hand glides across from the back of my head, down to my neck.

"You smell amazing," he tells me.

"Ha, that's still sweat from before."

"Yeah, but now it's sweat from this."

"Yeah, it is," I say and nibble on his lower lip, which he growls at.

"Naughty," he teases.

"I'm close babe," I inform him.

My words seem to add to his excitement, as he tightly squeezes his legs around my waist some more, encouraging me to go faster.

I pick up the pace, all whilst holding onto our kiss.

"Ugh… yes. Fuck!" He shouts and returns his lips to mine.

I can feel my climax ready to erupt. The sweat on my forehead drips off and lands on his face. His hand grips my wrist more tightly, too. He must be getting close to his orgasm.

Suddenly, the pace becomes too much for me to continue the kiss and my head nudges past his and my face is now buried in my pillow, right next to his neck.

"Oh, Mark. I'm close too," he reveals.

The grunts and heavy breaths continue to escape us as we both nearly finish.

I feel Kyle letting go of my wrists and now he places his hands on my ass cheeks. He grips them tightly for a moment, and then slaps my ass, which sets me off. I feel my body shudder and quake as I feel my climax to fruition.

Within a hot second, I feel my cock spurt ropes of cum inside the condom as I continue to thrust inside of Kyle.

"Ah, fuck!" I shout. My heavy breaths land on Kyle's neck.

My body continues to convulse. My orgasm still riding high.

All of this sets Kyle off, as his cock now erupts in between our chests. Most of his cum lands on his stomach and chest, but some of it reaches up to my stomach too.

"Argh. URGH." His moans make my ear lobes tremble.

A moment passes, and I lean further back, so that I can admire all of his body and see the result of what just happened between us. The end of this precious and special moment we just shared.

We continue to breathe in fast, but after a minute, our breaths become shallower.

"That… was… huff. Amazing," he says.

"Yeah, ugh. It bloody was," I tell him.

He looks up at me, and seeing his eyes after what we just done, draws me back into him.

I lean over to him once more and go in for our hundredth kiss of the night. I've lost count on how many times we've kissed today.

"Fuck, you're amazing, Mark."

"I am happy to hear that," I say. "You were great too. I do not know how I held out for so long when you've got an amazing ass like that."

"Such a sweet talker," he says.

I turn on my back and simply lie next to my amazing best friend, who is now my boyfriend.

We lay silently next to each other for a few minutes, but what feels like forever in a good way. I think we're both taking in the moment and realising how far we've come and how much has changed between us.

Kyle turns his body closer to me, so we're now face to face. He slowly strokes my chest, and then motions his fingers around one of my nipples in a circular motion.

"I love you, Mark."

"I love you too, Kyle."

ON THE PITCH

With those words being spoken, Kyle nudges himself under my shoulder and rests his head near mine.

This. This is how I will always want our nights to end. My man by my side.

With us settled in this cosy position, we drift off into sleep.

Chapter 27
Mark

After a good night's rest, I wake up and see Kyle sleeping peacefully. He's still tucked under my arm, as if he hadn't moved at all from when he fell asleep.

I take a mental picture of the way he is right now. Seeing him like this brings me a sense of joy. Knowing that he feels he can rest on me now. That we are at a point in our relationship where we can be like this with each other.

With the summer sun shining through the small gaps in my blinds, I admire what little I can see outside of my window, and then turn back to admire my handsome boyfriend.

"Morning, gorgeous," I call to him. His eyes blink twice before he fully opens them.

"Morning to you too." He smiles. "Last night was great."

"It sure was," I respond.

I softly caress his nearest thigh. "I can't wait to do that again," I tell him.

"Me too. Your dick insertion skills are spectacular," he tells me, and his words get a laugh out of me.

"Ha, thanks. I'm happy my skills meet your standards," I finish speaking in a posh tone.

ON THE PITCH

"You get five stars, babe. If I had to write a review, it would be 'I highly recommend. Worked as expected and could keep up'. That good enough of a review for you?" "Ha, yes. Very much," I answer. "Maybe my dick insertion skills are required by other men."

"Nah ah. This," he says and grips my cock, "is all for me to play with."

"Well, you certainly are my favourite toy now. Besides, this," I squeeze his ass cheek, "is also for me to play with."

"You certainly owned this ass last night," he says to me.

He reaches forward towards me and lays a slow kiss onto my lips. It is a delicate kiss, and not hearing any other sound, but the two of us, brings a sense of peace. A kind of peace I want again and again with this man.

"Kissing you, Mark, is like kissing you for the first time again. I never get tired of it, and I never will."

He eases himself back to his original position, with his head resting on my shoulder once again. The both of us lying beside each other, enjoying the quiet moment.

Sharing this moment with him has got me to ponder on how the both of us have already expressed our love for each other. Saying 'I love you' to a partner normally takes time in the relationship, but we have both said it quite early in our relationship.

"What's on your mind, babe?" He asks me, and damn, he truly gets me if he can clearly tell something is on my mind.

"Kyle, the both of us have already said 'I love you' to each other and we have only been together as boyfriends for a short amount of time."

"And do you think we have both said it too quick?"

"Yes, but I don't think that's a bad thing. We both mean it. I love you," I tell him.

"And I love you." He tenderly lays his palm on my chest.

"It's just us saying such a heavy thing like that to one another came so easy for the both of us."

He leans up slightly with his face now above me to my side. "Oh, Mark. You're a smart man, but sometimes you can be quite clueless. It's obvious why declaring our love for each other came so easy. It's because we have been best friends for a very long time, and we both fancied the other before we started dating."

I nod in agreement, but I feel like I am missing a piece of the puzzle. As if there is some other reason it all came so easy to us.

"Think of it this way, Mark," he says and nudges closer to me. "We were attracted to one another long before we came out and became a couple. With us being such a good friends, lifelong friends at that, I think once we opened ourselves up as a couple, the feelings that were already there for each other exploded. The love I had for you, and the love you had for me, came out so quick and fast because the love had always been there."

"Wow", I simply say. His explanation is so on point, and the way he said it has got my heart fluttering. He seems to have that effect on me with whatever he says or does. "Damn. That was beautiful, Kyle. You sure have a way with words." I brush his cheek and he leans into my touch, which I find adorable.

"Well, thanks," he says and kisses me on the lips. The touch of his lips has my heart continuing to flutter. Feelings of butterflies tighten in my stomach as the kiss lingers on.

ON THE PITCH

I cup his cheek again and take in his scent that gets me intoxicated with him even more.

"I would love to carry on with this, but we have to get out of bed at some point," he tells me and raises himself off the bed.

He reaches for his phone and turns it on. A few seconds later, and he checks his notifications.

"Ugh," he grunts, and I can tell he is not happy.

"What is it?" I ask.

"I've got a message from Jake. What does he want now?"

He clicks on the message and takes a moment to read it, his brow frowning as he does so.

"What did he say?"

"He said he's sorry about his outburst at our last practice session but would like to apologise in person."

A glint of happiness rises in me now that Jake has apologised to Kyle. I hope this means our team can go back to the way it was before.

"That's great to hear he apologised."

"Yeah, it is. I'm going to ask him if he wants to meet up today."

"Good," I simply say.

I see Kyle quickly type on his phone and he sends another message to Jake. Quickly, Kyle receives a reply in no time.

"He said he's up for meeting me today," Kyle tells me.

"Nice," I say to him.

I walk towards my wardrobe and pick out my clothes for today.

"Do you want to come with me?" He asks.

"I would, but I think it might be best if you just go. We don't know the reason why he was being funny with you that day, and he may feel tag teamed against if I come along. Besides, I plan on arranging those interviews we promised to James." I see Kyle's eyes light up upon hearing my words. "Shit. I forgot about that."

"Ha, well getting fucked good by your boyfriend is a good reason you forgot," I say to him.

"Who says the fucking was good?" He teases me, and I roll up my pyjama shirt and throw it at him.

"Ass," I call him, and he lets out that soft laugh of his that I adore so much.

Kyle puts his football uniform back on as they were the only clothes that he brought with him to my place. Seeing him in his kit gets my cock tingling. Something about his muscled, toned, slim, athletic build in our team's clothes gets me going, and I think he knows as he gazes down to my crotch.

"You horny fuck," I call out.

"Hey, when I see my sexy boyfriend getting a hard on, it's only natural for me to look at it and want to play with it."

"You can play with some other time," I say, and he pouts.

"When will the next time be?" He asks me as he gently presses a hand against my dick and kisses my neck.

"Oh, fuck. Soon," I say with hardly any breathing space between words. His touch and kiss has got me so hot and feeling flushed.

A few minutes pass and I am seeing Kyle at my front door and open it for him. "Will I see you tonight?" I question him, hoping he says yes.

"Of course."

"Good."

A moment goes by where we just stare into each other's eyes and we both reach out to each other, and kiss. The soft touch from his lips pulls me in more towards him. The sounds coming from our lips tingle my ears. Kissing him comes so easily to me, but pulling away and ending the kiss doesn't.

I have dreamt about kissing him for a long time, so I will relish in every chance I get to feel his lips pressed against mine.

"I could do this all day," he says to me and leans back.

"Same," is all I say, and I can see his lips curling into a wide smile, and I smile back at him.

"See you tonight then." He says as he walks out.

"See you later on, and that ass of yours."

He shakes his ass from side to side upon walking through my front garden and turns his head to wink at me. Such a tease.

Chapter 28
Kyle

I had such a great start to the day. Waking up next to Mark after we spent the night together was such a joyful and pleasant way to wake up. And then I got a text from Jake. As soon as I saw he messaged me, I felt a bit annoyed and thought that the good, spirted mood I was in would quickly evaporate. But no. Jake apologised about his behaviour to me and now I am on my way to the coffee shop we agreed to meet at, since he wants to apologise in person too. Maybe he will even explain his odd behaviour and outburst at the last practice session.

After parking my car and walking to the coffee shop, I step inside the building and spot Jake sitting at a small table in a corner. Good. He picked a good, secluded spot. Better to talk in private at the back corner instead of in the centre where most of the other customers are at.

"Hi, Jake." I stick my hand out and hope he accepts the warm handshake.

"Hey, Kyle," he says and gently shakes my hand. Good. We are off to a pleasant start. "What would you like to drink? I'll pay for us both. It's the least I can do."

I take a second to give him my answer as I was not expecting him to offer to pay. "I'll have a medium latte."

"Okay then," he says and gets off his seat and walks to the counter and orders our drinks.

A few minutes later, he arrives back at the table. "Here you go," he says as he sets down our drinks on the table. The steam from our drinks rises in the middle between us.

"Thanks for agreeing to meet me, Kyle. I appreciate it."

I can tell by the slight shakiness in his hands that he is indeed nervous about this. He almost spilt his coffee and my latte when walking back to our table.

"Jake. Breathe. Take it easy," I say to him. He must not realise how nervous he looks, as he seems surprised by my words.

"Will do, Kyle. I'm just a little nervous, is all."

He takes a moment to settle himself, and he slowly breathes in deeply. Then exhaling out with his eyes closed.

"I needed to do that. Thanks for the suggestion," he says to me.

"No problem. Since you're nervous, maybe it wasn't the best idea to get a hot cup of coffee. You should have gone for a bottle of water instead."

My words seemed to have put him in a better mood, more so than the slow breathing he did a second ago, as he lets out a small laugh and smiles.

"Ha, yeah, I should have gone for the water."

A moment passes by with no words being spoken, and we both use that chance to take a sip from our drinks.

"That is one tasty latte. Thanks for paying," I say.

"No problem, Kyle. Again, I owe you it for how I snapped at you."

"Speaking of which, shall we talk about that now?"

He swallows hard, and I see that nervous look in his eyes return, but only for a few seconds.

"Yes. Let's talk about that. First, I want to apologise in person like I said I would. So, Kyle. I am sorry for snapping at you at the practice session and being a dick. Then continuing that behaviour and letting it affect my playing during the match we had yesterday. I shouldn't have let it get that far. Not that it should have happened, anyway. I am sorry."

He lays his arms out on the table when he says sorry for the last time. I can tell he is being genuine. But I can also detect that there is a hint of sadness in his words, and his eyes when he looks at me.

"Apology accepted, Jake." I beam a hearty smile at him, letting him know I am fine with him now, instead of just relying on my words to accept his apology.

"Great. I am glad to hear that in person, Kyle. Hearing that from you has me feeling much better now. So, thanks."

He takes another sip from his coffee, and I do the same with my latte. The both of us savouring the taste of our drinks. We both linger the cups on our lips and put our drinks back on the table.

"So, it is time for me to explain the reasoning behind my behaviour," he tells me. A serious look overtakes him, and he perches his elbows on the table, leaning slightly closer to me.

"I'm gay too, Kyle."

Immediately, I am thrown off by his statement. I was definitely not expecting to hear that, but I am left more curious why him being gay has anything to do with his behaviour towards me lately.

Before I can even question him, he follows up by saying, "I saw the way you and Mark were looking at each other. I realised you were attracted to each other, and I know this sounds stupid, but seeing the two of you like that had me feeling jealous."

Jake's words continue to surprise me. I knew none of this. Though, I remember him looking back at me and Mark on that day.

He stops speaking for a moment, and downs a big sip, and then swallows hard.

"So, Jake. Were you angry because I seemed happy with Mark? Perhaps because you aren't out yet or don't have a partner?" I ask him calmy and try to be as gentle as possible.

"Yes," he answers. "But there is more to it than just that. To be honest, if it was just that, I wouldn't have been angry at you. Instead, I probably would have been making playful jokes about you and Mark."

He puts his head back, and a worrying expression forms on his face. I see him take in a deep breath, and slowly breathe out.

"Ok. Here goes." I'm not sure if he's telling me that or himself. I am going to go with the latter.

"So, a few years ago, my parents got divorced. It was a horrible divorce too. They were at each other's throats during the entire process. It was a shock to see, because there was no hint of anything bad going on between them. They got on so well with each other. Well, at least I thought they did."

My heart aches for him when he stops speaking briefly. I can tell this is a sore subject for him, and that he is still hurting from whatever happened during this time in his life.

"My parents were fighting over custody of me. Whose house I should spend more time at during the week and on weekends. All that kind of stuff."

Jake is one of the younger players on the team, at eighteen. So I am not too surprised if his parents were arguing about a custody agreement a few years ago.

"They eventually agreed on an agreement were I spend one week with mum, and then the next week with my dad. And that was fine for a while. I actually came to enjoy it once I came to terms with them divorcing."

Another sad look appears on his face, with a frown facing me.

"At some point," he continues, "my mum got with another man, not long after the divorce was over. This man had two other kids, and my mum started spending way more time with her boyfriend and step-kids. She tried forcing me into this new dynamic, when I was still grieving the loss of the old dynamic: me, dad, and mum."

"Man, I am sorry to hear that, Jake," I tell him. I know the importance of having a good and supportive family. Knowing that his family broke up, has me aching for him. I don't know what I would do if my family broke up, especially during my teenage years.

"Thanks, but it gets worse, unfortunately." He looks around and scans the room before talking again, almost making sure not too many people hear him, I guess. "After trying to force the families to blend, and realising I wasn't ready for that, my mum didn't care for me anymore. She took her boyfriend and kids on days out, and posted the photos online, with captions mentioning having a nice day out and spending time with her family. That fucking hurt."

"Damn. That is shitty," I say.

"Eventually, I started spending more time with my dad. Even staying at his place during the weeks I was supposed to be at my mum's. That went well for a while. My dad was much better than my mum by spending quality time with me after the divorce. But sadly, that ended too. He met a woman who he was spending more time with, but he still included me sometimes. Eventually, his new girlfriend found out I was gay, and started making jokes and remarks about my sexuality. My dad tried to get her to stop at first, but not much. She continued her remarks, and my dad did nothing about it. I felt betrayed by both my parents. I fucking hate how they treated me."

My heart breaks for Jake even more. I can feel the hate and sadness coming from him when he spoke his last few words. Having your family break apart and then abandoned by his parents must be incredibly difficult. And to make it worse, his dad let his girlfriend off with her awful comments. Disgusting.

"Jake, I am sorry."

"Don't be." He cuts me off and waves a hand. "I'm the one who bottled my feelings and lashed out at you. I am the one who is sorry."

"If you ever need to talk about anything, Jake, I am all ears. Mark will be too. I know that for sure. "

"Thanks, Kyle. I appreciate that. I am currently seeing a therapist. She has been a big help. In fact, after blowing up at you, I had to address my behaviour with her, and my therapist helped me see through my emotions."

"I am glad to hear that, Jake." He seems much more cheerful now that he has unloaded his baggage and explained himself. I'm glad to have my teammate back.

We chat for a while longer. Topics ranging from football, coming out, and which celebrities we find attractive.

"Thanks for seeing me, Kyle. I feel so much better now that we have spoken," he says to me.

"No problem. Take care, and remember if you need to talk about anything, just let me know."

"Will do," he says, and we both exit the coffee shop and walk in different directions, with me heading back to my car.

***

I arrive at Mark's place as he texted me to meet him there for the interviews we agreed to do when we spoke to James, after the last match we played.

"Thanks for agreeing to the interview, fellas. They were superb. You both gave insightful answers about what it's like being a gay man playing in football," James says to us over a video call.

"Awe, thanks James," Mark says. "We enjoyed talking with you."

"We sure did. This was fun," I say.

"Well, I am glad to hear that you two enjoyed this, and as a thank you gift, I have a hotel booking code for you two. It's for a hotel of your choosing that is based around the gay village in Manchester. The code is for a discounted price. How does that sound?"

Me and Mark both turn to each other in shock. It seems like we are going to Manchester.

"That sounds great, James," I say.

"Yeah, this is wonderful," Mark expresses.

"The pleasure is all mine. It brings me joy every time I see people smile when I tell them about the gift. Now, I will email you the instructions and the list of hotels, and you two just need to respond with the dates for your stay, and I will book everything."

ON THE PITCH

Mark holds my hand. His grip is shaky, as is mine, since we are both filled with excitement. We are now going on an unexpected trip to Manchester. This will be our first trip as a couple. I am looking forward to it.

"Thanks again for the interview fellas, and enjoy your stay in Manchester," James says right before ending the video call.

"Well, it seems we're going to the big ole gay village in Manchester," I say to Mark.

"Yeah. Our first couple's trip. How exciting," he says to me.

He kisses me on the lips and pulls away with a big, wide smile on his face. "We better get packing then," he says.

My heart flutters and a bolt of joy springs through me.

We're going on our first trip as a couple. It's going to be so wonderful. I know it will be.

Chapter 29

Mark

'You have arrived at Piccadilly Station.'

We hear the announcement welcome our arrival, as we step off the train. We are now in Manchester.

Feelings of excitement and suspense travel through me, as I look forward to what me and Kyle will do on our first trip as boyfriend and boyfriend. I still can't believe we're boyfriends.

"You ready?" I ask him from his side. I gently graze his nearest hand. A sense of fulfilment and wonder flow through me when I feel his touch.

"Yes," he answers, and turns his face to me. His rosy smile beams brightly.

We show our tickets to security, and then bustle through the crowds of other passengers and tourists, and soon we feel the fresh air. The city centre is now in view.

"Sure is busy," I remark.

"Yeah. Let's just go straight to the hotel first, and then do some exploring," Kyle advises.

"Good thinking. My arms are already tired from holding the luggage."

ON THE PITCH

Kyle laughs. "Come on, muscle man," he squeezes my right bicep. "Some luggage surely can't tire you already."

"Hey, you've got the lighter stuff," I say to him.

"That's because I packed lightly. We're only here for a few days, but you've seemed to have packed for a week. Way too many clothes you've brought with you." He lifts his bag in the air, teasing me with how light it is.

"Well, I packed my coat and thicker clothes in case it rains. It maybe summer, but I know it rains a lot here in Manchester."

"Fair enough," he says with gentle breath.

We continue walking through the city. Thanks to James, we got a big discount for our hotel booking.

The sounds of engines, car horns and people walking continue throughout the city. No matter where we turn, we can hear those same sounds. That is until we turn into a street, where the noise becomes quieter.

As we walk further into this street, we realise we are now in the famous Canal Street. The heart of the gay village in Manchester.

The both of us stop in place and turn to look at each other, and smile with glee now that we are here. We hold hands, and resume walking down the street. Pride flags and banners dangle above us and we can see more in the windows of the bars to our right. This sure feels like a welcoming place, and I cannot wait to make fresh memories here with Kyle.

We arrive at the hotel and quickly check in and make our way to the hotel room we are staying at.

"Wow. This looks great," Kyle calls out, and he's not wrong. The room is pristine and elegant, and the bed duvet is a dark red, with bronze stripes that fit in well with the clear, lightly shaded walls. The ensuite bathroom is nice and clean to, with the silver of the sinks and shower sparkling, and the mirror clear and spotless.

"The view isn't the best," I point out.

"Oh, you're right," Kyle says when he stands next to me. "We are in the city centre, so this isn't surprising."

"True," I simply agree.

A couple of hours later, after unpacking and exploring parts of the city, we decide to head to a restaurant for our evening meal.

The restaurant is busy with business people, groups, and other couples alike. The interior sparkles brightly, with a combination of the lights and the tables, cutlery and mantle pieces sparkling.

After we order our food, I take a moment to eye my gorgeous boyfriend. The short sleeve, black button-up shirt he's wearing hugs his body nicely. Accentuating his toned physique. He's also wearing light blue denim jeans that he knows are tight around his ass. Now I know why he insisted on walking in first. It's moments like this that make me realise what a lucky man I am to have fallen in love with my best friend, and to be Kyle's boyfriend.

"Hey, what you checking out?" he asks me.

"Oh, you know. Just my sweet, handsome boyfriend," I answer.

His cheeks blush and it's adorable to see, as always.

I just want to reach out to him and kiss him so sweetly right now, but that can wait until we get back to the hotel. Though I am going to find the wait tough.

The waiter brings our food to us, and we politely thank her.

With the slow, easy-going music playing on in the background, and the smell of food teasing our noses, we eat.

ON THE PITCH

Our first romantic meal in a restaurant couldn't be more delightful and perfect. Sitting across from Kyle, may be be such a small thing to many. But to me, it is a gift I will never stop cherishing. Anytime I get to look back into his eyes, it will always be a wonderful experience. Hearing his voice and enjoying his company is something I will forever cherish.

I truly am the luckiest man in the world. And it's all because of him.

Chapter 30
Mark

"Nice. The sun is out today. The perfect weather to do some sight-seeing and relax in Sackville Gardens." Kyle says to me after he opens the curtains to the window.

"It sure is a nice day indeed," I reaffirm when I stand by him, and rest my hands on his waist, and my chin on his shoulder. Taking in his morning scent. The smell of the shower gel he used last night after we came back from the restaurant, still lingers on him. I take a whiff, and hope he doesn't notice, but he does. "What are you doing?" He asks as he scratches my chin.

"Just smelling my handsome boyfriend."

"Why?"

"Because you smell gorgeous. Can't a man smell his boyfriend?"

"He can," he says. "Tonight, after we fuck, I want to smell every inch of you," he tells me.

"Who says we're fucking tonight?" I tease him with a smile.

"Ah, come on. We have to fuck each other's brains out on our first trip as a couple."

"I know. Besides," I pull him to me by his waist. My hands now cupping his ass. "I really want to play with this again." I lightly tap each cheek.

ON THE PITCH

"Good. Because I've really been wanting to play with my new favourite toy again." He gently strokes my shaft over the fabric of my pyjama shorts. He bites his lower lip and looks right at me in the eyes. We kiss and pull away to end the foreplay. We can continue this tonight after our day out in the city.

After we have had our breakfast and morning coffee, we quickly get dressed and begin exploring the city centre of Manchester.

We take a boat trip that was booked by James, which was a surprise since we didn't know he booked it until a couple of days before we arrived. That was nice of him to do.

The boat trip lasts an hour, and after that we head further into the city on foot, where we see a statue of Abraham Lincoln. We were both surprised to see that, as a statue of him in Manchester, was not something we would ever expect.

We wander through the city, checking out some stores and visit the nearby shopping centre. Kyle was really in his element when we went clothes shopping. He's always relished in some retail therapy for as long as I have known him. Though back in our younger years, it was video games he wanted to buy. Now it's clothes he buys, and I am more than happy to buy him some gifts.

"Thanks, babe," he says to me.

"No problem, sexy," I say back to him.

We leave the shopping centre and make our way to Canal Street.

Once we arrive, we see a few people sitting at the tables across from the bars. We've come on a weekday, and it is early afternoon, so fortunately it isn't busy at all.

I collect our beverages after I ordered them and bring them to the table Kyle chose for us. It's a lovely spot he picked, as it is right beside the canal itself and overlooking Sackville Gardens. The lush green from the grass and trees is a pleasant sight to behold and makes for a nice backdrop for us as we drink and converse.

"Mmm, yum." Kyle takes his first sip of his red fruity drink. "This is very nice."

I take my first sip of the pineapple and mango drink I got, with a little umbrella hanging on the side of the glass. "Oooh, yeah. Very nice indeed," I mention after the taste lands on my tongue, and I swallow the juice.

I take a moment to admire Kyle. With his pink shorts and white tank top, his toned muscles are on show, and I am filled with a sense of pride, seeing the results of his time at the gym paying off. I certainly approve of his look.

"My eyes are up here," he calls out. Catching my gaze over him.

"Well, your sunglasses are covering your eyes, so I can't see them," I point out.

He laughs after taking another sip. "I've been checking you out through these shades."

"I knew it," I say and chuckle.

"I can never get enough of your big, muscular arms."

After he speaks, I flex my biceps and stroke one of them with my other hand.

"Oh, fuck," he whispers from across the table. "Don't tease me like that right now. I really don't want to get a hard-on with these shorts."

"Fine." I settle my arms back on the table.

"You're such a tease," he calls me and goes back to sipping his fruity drink.

ON THE PITCH

We finish our drinks, and a staff member collects the empty glasses and smiles at us. Canal Street really is a pleasant place.

With our hands holding on to each other's, we slowly walk through Sackville Gardens. We stop at each attraction, taking the time to appreciate each one. From the Beacon of Hope, which documents the history of AIDS, to the statue of a WW2 hero and the father of computer science, Alan Turing.

We sit beside the statue as it is also a bench and pose for the camera on Kyle's phone he set up.

With the picture now taken, we settle down on a patch of grass, with a large tree beside us providing some shade from the sun.

Feeling free and safe in this area, Kyle rests his head on my shoulder as we lay down on the dry grass. The sun beams through the small gaps of the leaves hanging above us from the tree. The warm breeze gently waves over us. I feel a little tingle sensation around my neck when it passes.

"Ah... This," Kyle breathes out. "This feels so right. Just you and me, right here, enjoying the peace and quiet."

He is spot on. This absolutely feels right. I never would have thought this would be happening. Having the man of my dreams on my shoulder, relaxing in such a beautiful area, but here we are. And I wouldn't have it any other way.

"I love you," he says, and he gently twists his fingers into mine.

"I love you too," I say and kiss his hand. The corners of his lips curve into a smile that just makes me want to kiss him properly right now.

"Kyle?"

"Yes."

"I am so glad that we crossed paths in our lives. I couldn't imagine what my life would have been like without you in it."

Slowly, he raises his head and chest up, and turns to me with the same smile he showed me a few seconds ago.

"Same here, Mark. There is no other man out there who I could love more than you. You're my rock. My soul mate. The love of my life."

After he speaks his words, he resumes resting on me and we're like that for some time before we decide to head back to the hotel.

We get up and cut through Canal Street one more time, as tomorrow we will be returning home.

A couple of hours after we have had our afternoon dinner, the summer sky goes dim, and it's time for me and Kyle to have some more fun again. We've been teasing each other enough throughout the day.

"I believe we should have some fun right now," Kyle whispers in my ear from behind. We have only been back in our hotel room for a few minutes, and the fun is already starting.

I turn to meet his gaze and say, "I agree. I'll get the lube. You go on ahead in the bedroom."

He takes a step back from me and drops his shorts and takes his tank top off. He dons a sexy smirk, and he turns around to show me his pale, bubbly ass and gives it a smack.

"Fuck, your ass looks good," I tell him.

"Well, it's all yours to play with," he says with a wink, and walks into the bedroom.

When he's out of sight, I strip my clothes off and drop them in the same spot of his and grab the bottle of lube. I walk to the bedroom and see that he is already on all fours on the bed. His ass facing me as soon as I enter the room.

"Come on. Give your boyfriend what he wants," he teases me some more, and slaps his ass once again.

I get on my knees behind him on the bed, and with a drop of lube on my index finger, I dab it around his hole.

"Oh," he lightly gasps when the coldness of the gel touches him.

I use two fingers after putting more lube on them and apply it in circular motions around his anus. After getting him ready, I place some lube on my cock, and slowly edge the tip inside of him.

"Ahh," he moans again. With both hands, I grab him by the waist, keeping him steady as I ease every inch of my cock in him.

"Is that alright for you?" I ask, hoping he isn't in discomfort.

"Yes. It feels good," he answers after taking in a gasp of air.

"Good."

Now that I know he feels fine, I slowly thrust my pelvis, causing my cock to push back and forth inside of him. Though I am starting easy, by taking only a few inches out of him, and then back in.

"Ahh... oh, yeah," he mumbles. His shallow words tickle my ears, and a sense of fulfilment flows through me, knowing that I am making him feel good and pleasing him.

"You feel so good, babe," I tell him. I ease my upper body over his back, and place my head just above his, and pick up the pace with my pelvic movements. Judging by his moans and yells of pleasure, he is certainly enjoying this, and I am enjoying giving it to him.

"Oh, god. Keep at it, Mark." He breathes in deep and exhales in between thrusts. "Fuck, this feels so good. You make me feel so good."

He turns his gaze to tell me that last part, and I smile back and thrust back inside of him, hard.

"Oh, YES!" He yells out.

I ease off momentarily and gently shift his legs further out by pushing them with mine. I then place my hands on his shoulders. Keeping him steady and holding him closer to me, causing him to arch his back a little.

I pick up where I left off and enter inside of him again.

"Yes, yes. Oh, my."

"I love hearing you like this, babe," I tell him, and smack his ass in the same spot he spanked himself earlier on.

His moans continue to stimulate my hearing. His loud gasps of pleasure are becoming just as enjoyable to me as my cock stroking in and out of him.

We continue this position for a few more minutes, and then I sense my orgasm coming to fruition.

"I'm getting close, babe. I'm gonna cum," I reveal to him.

I want to look him in the eyes and kiss his lips when I cum, so I pull out of him, and with my hands, guide him to turn on his back. His legs spread to the side of mine. Quickly, I resume fucking him again. Though this time, I would say we're not just fucking, but making love.

I motion my cock in and out of him with slow strokes and clasp his hands with mine. The soft touch of his fingers sends a shiver down my arms. His touch is electric to me. Simple acts, like touching his hands, take on a whole new significance for me. I can't get enough of him. He's all I want for the rest of my life.

With my chest now just inches above his, I lean my head down and kiss his sweet lips. Our lips fit together so well at this point. Every time we kiss, it keeps getting better. Keeps getting sweeter and more intimate. Our tongues clash with one another, and I can tell my climax is seconds away.

Kyle lets go of my left hand and places his on the back of my head. My pelvic movements become unsteady as my orgasm nears. I become unsteady myself, and my head pushes to the side, breaking the kiss, and I feel it. My cock spurts cum deep inside of Kyle, and we both grunt loudly.

"Argh, ugh. Yes. Ohhh, fuck," I moan near his ear.

"Yes. Yes. Oh, god," he breathes near my left ear. I continue humping him as cum is still shooting from my cock. Round after round of cum, all going inside of him.

Soon, my orgasm ends, and I fall completely on Kyle's chest and stomach, and that's when I feel something wet between us. He also came, and the contents of his orgasm shot all over his torso region.

I lift my head up and look down below between us, then look back at him, and we both laugh lightly.

The moment passes, and we are still looking deep into each other's eyes.

Steadily, I lower my lips to his and kiss him once more. He wraps both his hands around me, and gyrates his hips, stimulating my now spent cock.

Moments like this make me realise just how lucky I am to have this wonderful man, who I am honoured to call my boyfriend, in my life. This connection we have is not something I could ever find with someone else. He is the one person in life who could ever make me feel the way I do when I am with him. With all of my heart, I will love him till the day I die. I will try to make his life happy and enjoyable, because he does that for me by just being next to me. I love him and I always will.

I settle beside him, and he snuggles up next to me, and he lays his head on my shoulder. He places a hand on my chest, and I wrap my left arm around him.

We slowly breathe in and breathe back out. The quietness takes over, and we say nothing. We simply enjoy the peace after being close with one another.

Chapter 31
Kyle

"How was your trip to Manchester, fellas?" Mark's dad, Peter, asks us.

We're at his parents' back garden and enjoying their BBQ cooking, along with my parents, Mark's sister Amy, and our friend Sarah. A big family gathering just for the fun of it. It's wonderful.

"It was great," Mark answers. "We had a good time."

"We really did. Canal Street and Sackville Gardens are wonderful spots to visit," I tell Peter.

"I'm glad to hear that, boys," he says and smiles warmly at us. He places an arm around Mark's neck, embracing his son. "And I am glad to see you being this happy," he says to Mark. "And I am thankful for you, Kyle, for making him feel that way." He raises his glass to me, and I can't help but feel warm and touched by his words. He truly appreciates me, and what I mean to his son.

"Thank you, Peter." I tip my head to him and raise my glass to his.

"Awe. My boyfriend and dad getting along. How nice to see." Mark is smiling so cheerfully, and it just adds to my heartfelt state right now, witnessing this moment.

Peter gets back to cooking the chicken wings at the BBQ, and we pace ourselves over to where my parents are talking to Mark's mum,

Rebecca. My mum and dad are cracking jokes with Rebecca and discussing moments about when me and Mark were children.

"He was a right show off, always trying to get everyone's attention," my mum states about my younger self.

"Well, that certainly is true, even now. He's always trying to get attention," Mark chimes in, and softly nudges me with his elbow.

"Hey, I got your attention. You should be thankful for my need to be seen," I say. Everyone laughs around us after hearing my words.

"Mark was the opposite. He was a completely shy as a child," Rebecca informs us. "But that changed as he got older. When he first started working out, I thought he just wanted to build muscle for the ladies. How wrong was I?" she finishes, and the laugher comes back from all of us. Even Peter, as he continues to man the BBQ.

We continue to converse, drink, and crack jokes. I am completely soaking in all this positivity and love right now in this moment. It feels great. Me and Mark being open as a couple to our families and a good friend. We both posted photos of us on social media, and our teammates posted nice positive comments. Even Jake, which was nice to see.

"So," Sarah catches my attention. "Have you two thought more about that trip I mentioned? About going somewhere with hunks on the beach."

"Oh, yes," I say in wonder, and smile hard at the imagery those words conjure in my head. "We haven't much, but I think we should. What do you think?" I turn to Mark, anticipating his response to this idea.

"A trip abroad somewhere sunny and nice, with my gorgeous boyfriend, surrounded by other hunky men and both of us checking them out. Of course I want to do this. It's sound like an amazing holiday."

We are both smiling hard now over the prospect of this holiday we have in mind.

"Well, when you see these hunky men on the beach, remember that I was the one who suggested it. I expect to be rewarded handsomely for my idea," Sarah jokes, and continues laughing.

"Food is ready," Peter calls out. The rest of us get off our seats and walk over to Peter, ready to enjoy the delicious smelling food he has cooked for all of us.

"Cheers Pete," my dad says, and others say something similar to him. All appreciating the effort Peter put in.

"My darling husband. The amazing cook he is," Rebecca says, and pecks him on the cheek with her lips.

We eat the delicious food, with the sun shining brightly over us on the decking. This couldn't be more perfect. Me and Mark together, spending time with our families and Sarah, enjoying the good food and each other's company.

This is my life right now, and I couldn't be any happier.

I look over at Mark and show him a smile. He smiles back after taking a bite out of a wing. He laughs upon realising that, and that makes my heart flutter for him as usual.

I love this man with all my heart. He is the best thing that has ever happened to me, and I will cherish him for the rest of my life.

Epilogue - Kyle

"Wow! What a hunk he is," I call out to Mark. We're sitting on sun lounges, on a beach in Sitges, Spain. Enjoying the sun and the hunks that pass us by.

"Oh, god, you're right. He is fit," my boyfriend says in a hushed, but excited tone.

"It's good that we remembered to bring our sunglasses. We don't want to be squinting our eyes when checking these fit fellas out."

"That's for sure," he says back to me. "Though I've got the hottest fella right next to me." He lowers his sunglasses and winks at me.

"Oh, how cheesy you are sometimes. I love it," I tell him.

So we got our scenery of hunks on the beach after all. I am going to have to thank Sarah for the suggestion when we get back home.

"Damn," Mark says. I know he is referring to the cute sun-tanned man who is jogging in tight speedos.

"Hey, my ass is better." My words snap his attention back to me.

"I know it is, babe, and I am so lucky to enjoy it."

His smooth words and cute eyes make me blush at him. "That you are."

"And you're lucky for getting to ride this," he gestures to his impressive physique and then his groin.

ON THE PITCH

"That I am."

The jokey banter between us distracts us from the view, and we both just smile hard at each other.

I eye his groin area as he is packing a hard bulge right now. "I see you're liking the hunks on the beach," I point out.

"Hey, you said to me back at the hotel, that as long as I park in the correct spot, you don't mind where I get my motor running."

"That I did. And tonight, I hope you park that again in me," I say and nod my head to his dick.

"Of course," he says so cheerfully.

We both turn on our backs on the sun lounges and stare out at the beach again. Taking in the sunlight's view beaming over the sea and the water glistening. The warm breeze we feel brushes over our bare chests. It's wonderful. It's beautiful. But what makes this even more delightful is the man I get to enjoy this moment with.

This moment wouldn't be nowhere near as magical if I wasn't sharing it with him. His presence makes everything much more impactful and wonderful. Until I loved him, I never knew I could feel this way at all. Mark really has unlocked new emotions for me, and only he could do that. No one else could. Only him.

I am looking forward to living with him full time when we go back home, as we will rent a house together for the first time.

"As much as I am enjoying this holiday with you, Mark. I cannot wait to go back home and move in together."

"Me too, babe. It's going to be great living together."

We smile once more at each other. Knowing what awaits for us back home. Us moving forward as a couple and in life.

I reach for my glass by my side in the space between us, and he does the same. We both hold our glasses up and click them together.

"To new beginnings," he says.

"And to us," I say back.

We both take a sip and put down our glasses and lay back down. Enjoying the afternoon sun.

"Here," I hear him say. He reaches his hand out to mine. I do the same and hold his hand. His gentle touch is something I will forever cherish. It's comforting for me. When I feel it, I know I am safe and loved.

"I love you, Kyle, and I always will. I will forever be thankful we crossed paths in our lives."

"I love you, Mark. And I look forward to spending the rest of our lives together. It's going to be wonderful."

We both turn our heads and gaze at each other, with our hands still holding onto each other's.

This is love, and I am fortunate to experience it like this and it's all thanks to him. My soulmate. My life partner.

My best friend.

NOTE FROM THE AUTHOR

Thanks for reading, and I hope you enjoyed it.

Please consider leaving a review on Amazon. Reviews help out a lot and I would appreciate it. Also, kindly mention about this book to others who you think maybe interested in reading it. Word of mouth helps out to.

Thanks again.

If you enjoyed this book and want to know when the next book in The Majestic Lions series is out, or any other books I will write, consider following me on social media to stay informed.

Social links below to follow me

@michaelmabelauthor on Instagram

Michael Mabel on Facebook

Also, check out my Amazon Author Profile, on the store front.

My debut novella

Two Hearts, One Business: An MM Office Romance Novella

If you enjoyed reading this book, you may like my debut novella. It features a clean, blossoming romance between the boss of the business and an employee. It ends with a happily ever after.

Blurb for Two Hearts, One Business: An MM Office Romance Novella

<u>Nick</u>

As heir to and CEO to Charwood Enterprises, I have become accustomed to a certain lifestyle. I know my charm and looks, combined with my fortune, have made me desired by many people. But many of these people I meet, only befriend me to boost their social image and piggyback off my fortune. I'm done with it. I simply want to make a genuine connection with people Yet, I feel my fortunate upbringing and wealth, seem to push the genuine caring people away from me, and invite the people who just want to use me. I just want someone to be with me, for who I am as a person. Someone I can cuddle and spend the nights with. Settle down and enjoy life together. I simply desire one thing. Love.

***

<u>James</u>

I have been working for the company for many years now and though I am happy that my hard work has paid off, it has come at the cost of not doing normal stuff people my age have done by now. I'm twenty-seven, yet I have never been in a relationship, I don't have much of a social life. Heck, I have never been kissed. All because I have buried my head in studies and work. Working hard for success, so that my life never goes back to the way it was when I was in foster care. I have finally had enough. I want excitement. I want to have fun and know what it's like to spend time with someone special. I want to feel butterflies when I receive a text from a boyfriend. Make plans and do all that cute stuff that couples do. I want to start living a life of happiness and fulfilment.

Michael Mabel

Michael Mabel is a British self-published author, who enjoys reading and writing MM romance. Stories about men finding love, companionship with other men, in many different scenarios.